BY AWARD WINNING AUTHOR
TELL COTTEN

YANCY

BOOK FIVE
IN THE LANDON SAGA

A SOLSTICE WESTERN

Yancy

Tell Cotten

Also by Tell Cotten

(The Landon Saga Books)
Confessions of a Gunfighter
Entwined Paths
Cooper
Rondo

Dedication
To my brother, Justin

Illustrator: Bill Olivas
www.billolivas.com
wbolivas@yahoo.com

Cover design:
Marcy Meinke/Converse Printing & Design
www.ConversePrinting.com
mike@converseprinting.com

Publisher's Note:

This is a work of fiction. All names, characters, places, and
events are the work of the author's imagination.

Any resemblance to real persons, places, or events is
coincidental.

Solstice Publishing - www.solsticepublishing.com

Author's note

YANCY has continued storylines from past books in The Landon Saga series. While it can be read as a stand alone, it is recommended that new readers start with the first book in the series, CONFESSIONS OF A GUNFIGHTER.

Prologue

The mule strained under the weight of the wagon. His hooves sank into the ground with each step, and progress was slow.

A tall, slender man sat in the seat, and his wife sat beside him. Their twelve-year-old son was behind, and he looked anxiously between them as they pulled into Midway.

There was only one main street, and it was long and dusty. There were some cattle pens at the end of town, and near the middle stood a big, fancy hotel. There were also a few livery stables, a sheriff's office, a general store, and a doctor's office.

There was a small house on the edge of town, and a man and a woman were sitting on the porch, drinking coffee. The man was tall, wide shouldered, and had a weathered look about him. As for the woman, she was small and slim. She had a sharp, young-looking face with long, brown hair.

They studied the wagon as it stopped in front of them. The wagon was worn, and had been patched several times, as had the canvas tarp. The wheels needed greasing, and the brake squeaked.

All three wore patched clothes, and the boy was bare headed.

"Morning," the man from the wagon said. "I'm Jack Walden. This is my wife, Suzan, and my boy, Wyatt."

"Cooper Landon," the man on the porch said. "This is Josie, my wife."

"Ma'am," Jack said.

Josie smiled and nodded.

"Where you headed?" Cooper asked.

"California."

"With only one mule?"

"We lost our other mule a few days back," Jack explained. "That's why we're here."

"A team of horses would be faster," Cooper suggested.

"Mules are cheaper," Jack said, and his face reddened a bit.

Cooper saw the embarrassed look, but he didn't acknowledge it.

"They are at that," he agreed.

"Would you know anybody in town that has a mule for sale?" Jack asked.

Cooper glanced at Josie and looked back at Jack.

"I've got a mule," Cooper announced. "We call him Jughead."

Jack's face filled with hope.

"Would you sell him?"

"I sure would."

"Is he broke for a wagon?"

"Should be."

"Is he gentle?"

Cooper's face reddened some.

"Sometimes."

"Can you ride him?"

Cooper frowned hesitantly, and Josie frowned at him.

"Sometimes," he said again.

Jack frowned thoughtfully. He glanced at his wife and looked back at Cooper.

"How much you want for him?"

Cooper squirmed in his chair as he thought on that.

"Five dollars?"

"I can pay a dollar," Jack said firmly.

Cooper didn't think for long.

"I'll take it."

Chapter one

In one way or another, I've been a lawman most of my adult life. It's one of the few things in life I'm good at.

I'm also mighty handy with my Colt six-shooter. Not to brag, but I've never been beat. Me being alive is proof of that.

Rondo Landon and Lee Mattingly are still alive too, and I know Lee likes to speculate on who's the best between us.

I reckon it's an interesting question for some, but I've never thought on it much.

My name is Yancy Landon. Like Rondo, I'm smaller than most, and I'm spry and in good shape. Some would call me handsome, although I'm not sure about that.

I've never been one for talking. I think that silence is often the best answer, but most folks never figure that out.

My older brother Cooper is the talker. Tall and wide shouldered, he has an easy-like way about him that I've often envied. Folks admire Cooper because of his character; only reason they admire me is because I'm good with a Colt.

I reckon that's partly the reason why I've never liked being around folks. Strangers always stare at me, hoping to see something, and that gets tiresome.

We Landons are a well-known family. And, we're also known for our mean temper during times of trouble.

However, it really isn't a temper. Instead, it's just a feeling we all get down deep inside.

It's a feeling of confidence, calmness, loneliness, sharp keenness, and pure meanness all rolled up into one. It also dulls the senses, and many a time we had been hurt and didn't even know it until afterwards.

Cooper and I have been riding together for a long time now. I was a lawman back east before the war, and Cooper was my deputy. Then the war broke out, and we joined the Union on the same day.

My name was well known by the time the war was over. We both received honorable discharges, and we came out west on a cattle drive.

It wasn't long until we were pulled back into service. I was promoted to Captain in the new Texas police force, and we were both assigned to Midway.

Mostly, the Texas police force was corrupt.

The purpose of the police force was supposed to be to fight crime and help with frontier defense, but in most towns that didn't happen. Instead, Governor Davis used his police force to arrest anyone that opposed him.

But I ignored his corrupt ways, and we did our best to treat the folks at Midway fairly. It wasn't easy. We had fought for the North, and there were a lot of folks that disliked us because of that.

J.T. Tussle, a salty old cowman, was one of those that disliked us. He had control of most of the range around Midway, but there were a lot of greedy cattlemen that wanted it. It was a tough fight, and by the time it was over we had finally gained the respect of Tussle and the other cowmen.

However, recently that respect had become a bit strained. A while back a stagecoach had been robbed, and a man named Stew Baine killed two men.

Coop and I tried our best, but it was Sergeant Wagons that actually found and killed Stew. He also saved the town from burning while I was gone looking for Cooper.

That made Sergeant Wagons an instant hero. The nickname 'The man who killed Stew Baine' stuck, and the local paper ran several stories about it. There was even talk that a dime novel was being written about it back east.

To make matters worse, Cooper brought back an Indian captive girl named Josie. Judge Parker married them a short while later, and there were some folks that didn't like that.

Coop and I were also shot up some, so we couldn't do much.

Soon as we got back on our feet, word came that Richard Coke had defeated Governor Davis in the election of 1874.

That was good news. However, that also brought an abrupt end to the police force, so Coop and I were out of a job.

Coop was especially worried about that. He and Josie had some money from selling some pelts, and they were planning on building a cabin. However, they didn't have enough money to finish it. Cooper needed steady paydays, and he reminded me of that often.

There was now no law in Midway, and I had hoped that the town council would offer me the sheriff's job. Instead, they decided to hold an election.

Sergeant Wagons and I both entered the election.

We had two weeks to campaign, but I didn't care for any of that nonsense. Folks already knew who I was, what I stood for, and how I ran things. I figured that was enough.

Sergeant Wagons took a different approach. He knocked on doors and gave speeches whenever possible.

I figured folks would get tired of being bothered, but for some reason they didn't seem to be. It was confusing, because I always got irritated whenever I was around Wagons for very long.

It was now the evening before the election.

The town was all stirred up, wondering who would win. It was a bit too much excitement for me, so I mainly stayed at the jail and drank coffee.

One more day, I thought, *until all this nonsense ends and I'm elected sheriff.*

Chapter two

That evening I sat out on the porch at the jail. Coop and Josie were off by themselves, busy planning their cabin.

I had just made a fresh pot of coffee. I poured myself a cup, and I put three spoonfuls of sugar in and stirred it with my finger.

I took a swig and sighed in contentment. It tasted sweet, and that's how I liked it.

It was almost dark when Judge Parker walked up.

"Evening, Yancy," he said.

"Judge," I nodded. "When did you get back?"

"Just a while ago," Judge Parker replied, and added, "I figured you might be here, drinking coffee."

"Sit," I offered. "Have some."

Judge Parker poured himself a cup and sat. It was silent as we drank our coffee.

Judge Parker was short and pudgy, with fat fingers. Whatever the situation, he always seemed to look distinguished and important.

We had known each other for a long time. He was a good judge, and we worked well together.

"How'd the trial at Empty-lake go?" I asked.

Judge Parker grunted.

"He escaped before I got there. Rondo and his two deputies took out after him, and one of the deputies killed him."

"Two deputies?" I raised an eyebrow. "Last I heard, Rondo only had one."

"Lee Mattingly was the other deputy," Judge Parker explained. "I believe it was a temporary arrangement."

I scowled as I thought on that.

"Lee Mattingly, a lawman? What's this world coming to?"

"It was a woman that helped Tanner escape," Judge Parker said. "Her, and an older man named Virgil Carson."

"Never heard of him."

"Rondo killed him. As for Lucy, she'll be an old woman by the time she gets out of Huntsville," Judge Parker said, and he added bitterly, "That is, if she doesn't escape."

I was confused by that last remark, but I didn't say anything.

"Too bad, Tanner getting killed," Judge Parker continued. "It would have been a big trial. Have you heard of Ike Nash?"

"Some," I nodded.

"Tanner was his son."

"What'd he do?"

"Killed a fella," Judge Parker explained.

I nodded, and it fell silent.

I could tell that Judge Parker had something on his mind, so I waited patiently.

"Ike Nash is more corrupt than Governor Davis was," Judge Parker finally declared.

"Why don't you send him to prison?"

"I can't. He has strong ties all the way back to Washington," Judge Parker said. "I can't touch him until he makes a mistake, and Ike doesn't make mistakes."

"I hear he's been buying up ranches all over Texas," I recalled.

"He's building his own little empire," Judge Parker agreed. "He's also involved in several businesses, all illegal. But, he's got it set up so that nothing can be traced back to him. I've even sent some of his men to prison, but then they escape."

"Huntsville?"

"It's happened twice now."

"Do you think he has a man inside?"

"Yes," Judge Parker said. "And, that ain't all. He's also been trading rifles to the Indians. Do you remember Wade Davis?"

"How can I forget," I said wryly, and I patted my shoulder where he'd shot me.

"He was working with Ike," Judge Parker declared. "I can't prove it, but I know. And now, Ike's got a new partner."

"Why are you telling me all this?" I narrowed my eyes.

Judge Parker took a swig of coffee before he replied.

"I want you to drop out of the sheriff's race," he announced.

I was startled, and I looked at Judge Parker and frowned. "What for?"

"Now that Governor Davis has been defeated, the Texas Rangers are being reorganized," Judge Parker explained. "I'd like for you and Coop to join up. You'd both answer to me."

"Doing what?"

"It's time for this country to unite, Yancy. The war's been over for several years, but men like Ike are still stirring up trouble," Judge Parker said, and declared, "I want to crush Ike. I want to crush his entire operation."

I frowned as I thought on that.

"I needed you before, and I need you again," Judge Parker said. "This is much bigger than the sheriff's job. This is a job that will take months, maybe even years. First, we've got to stop Ike from trading rifles to the Indians. After that, I want you to find out how his men escape from Huntsville. And then, after we've crushed his entire operation, we'll go after Ike himself."

"I'll have to think on it," I replied, and added, "Coop will have to make up his own mind. He and Josie have plans."

"Take a few days to think on it," Judge Parker said.

"Whatever we decide, I want to wait until after the election," I said.

"What for?"

"Because I want to win," I admitted. "I can always resign later and pick a replacement."

"Sergeant Wagons can't handle the job?"

"No," I replied. "He can't."

"Nobody else seems to know that," Judge Parker said. "What I hear, a lot of folks like him."

I grunted in response.

Judge Parker chuckled as he stood.

"Well, you and Coop talk it over. Let me know."

"We will," I nodded.

"And remember; this conversation never happened," Judge Parker warned. "Wrong folks in Washington find out about this, then we'll be in prison instead of Ike."

I smiled faintly and nodded.

"You want to win this election, you'd better get out tomorrow and kiss a few babies," Judge Parker suggested.

"I don't like babies."

Judge Parker chuckled and left. Meanwhile, I finished my coffee and went to find Cooper.

Chapter three

I found Cooper and Josie at a nearby café.

The café was very simple. It had a dirt floor, the tables were boards laid over barrels, and flies buzzed all around. But the food was good, and that's all that mattered.

Cooper and Josie were eating steak and beans, and I also noticed a fresh baked apple pie.

"Sit down," Cooper said as I walked up. "Join us."

"What are we celebrating?" I asked as I pulled up a chair.

"We're saying good-bye," Cooper announced.

"To who?" I frowned.

"Jug-head," Cooper explained, and Josie nodded. "I sold him this morning."

"Well, that is reason to celebrate," I said as I poured myself some coffee. I poured some sugar in, stirred, took a swig, and sighed in contentment. "I never did like that mule."

"Wade Davis would have probably rode right by me if it hadn't been for Jug-head," Cooper recalled.

"So, it's Jug-head's fault we both got shot," I surmised.

"I can't think of anyone else to blame," Cooper said.

"How 'bout Wagons?"

"He was still here," Cooper reminded.

"Jug-head it is then," I smiled.

I caught the waiter's attention. He came over, and I ordered steak and beans.

"Have you been hiding at the jail all day?" Cooper asked.

"I haven't been hiding," I frowned. "Matter of fact, I've been busy."

"Doing what?"

"I've been talking to Judge Parker," I declared.

"He's back? What did he have to say?"

16

"Plenty."

"Such as?" Cooper prompted.

"There's no hurry," I said. "We can talk later."

Cooper nodded thoughtfully. The waiter brought me my steak, and it was silent while we ate.

We were almost done when Sergeant Wagons burst in. Several of his supporters were with him, and they were all loud and cheerful.

They grabbed an empty table across the room, and it was then that Wagons spotted me. He grinned and walked towards us. Everyone in the room saw him, and it was suddenly very quiet.

Sergeant Wagons was only around twenty years of age. He was chubby with fair skin and red cheeks, and his clothes always seemed too small.

As I watched him, I couldn't help but wonder again how he had ever managed to kill Stew Baine.

"Hello, Yancy," he drawled.

"Sergeant."

"I'm not a Sergeant anymore," he reminded.

"No, you ain't," I forced a smile.

"You can call me Jason if you want."

"Wagons will do."

"Do you mind if I call you Yancy?"

"Yes."

Wagons hesitated, and I could tell that he didn't know what to say to that. So, he chose to ignore my remark.

"I've always liked you, Yancy," he said boastfully. "I hope there's no hard feelings between us. After the election, I mean."

"Depends."

"On what?" Wagons frowned.

"On who wins."

"You gonna be a sore loser, Yancy? I was hoping we could still be friends."

I laid my fork down and looked up at him.

"We've never been, and never will be, friends."

Wagons' face flushed.

"I'm sorry you feel that way, Yancy. I thought we always worked well together. You, me, and Coop accomplished a lot."

I glanced at Cooper. He was smiling, and I could tell that he was enjoying the confrontation.

"Whatever was accomplished," I said stiffly. "Wasn't accomplished together."

"Well, I reckon that is true," Wagons looked proud. "After all, I saved the town from burning, and I also killed Stew Baine. You and Coop were nowhere around."

"We were busy."

"Well, I reckon we know where we stand with each other," Wagons said. "I wish it wasn't this way."

"Sure."

"I hope we're not enemies after tomorrow."

"Like I said; it depends."

"We're both just trying to do what's best for this town," Wagons continued.

"No. You're trying to do what's best for you," I replied.

Wagons opened his mouth, couldn't think of anything to say, stood there a moment, and then turned and walked back across the room.

I glanced at Cooper and Josie. Josie was watching me with wide eyes, but Cooper was still grinning.

"'Ol Wagons is really getting under your skin, ain't he?" Cooper said.

I scowled as I took a swig of coffee.

"If he calls me 'Yancy' one more time," I warned, but didn't finish the sentence.

Chapter four

"Think you'll win this election?" Cooper asked me.

"We'll know tomorrow," I shrugged.

"You ain't even got a gut feeling?"

"No."

Cooper frowned, but didn't reply.

We had finished supper, and we were walking down the street towards our house. The sun had just disappeared in the west, and it was getting dark.

"We ain't discussed it, but what are we going to do if you don't win?" Cooper asked.

I didn't reply as I squinted ahead. There was something in the street in front of our house, but I couldn't make it out.

"That's what Judge Parker and I were discussing," I said.

Cooper thought on that before he said anything.

"Last time you and Judge Parker had a talk, we ended up here in the middle of a range war," Cooper recalled.

"We did," I nodded.

"Almost got us killed."

"True."

"I'm married now," Cooper pointed out.

"You are."

"That means I've got responsibilities to consider."

"It does," I agreed.

"Things ain't like they used to be, Yancy. I've got to start planning for the future."

"You do," I nodded.

Cooper looked at me and frowned.

"Have I ever told you how irritating it is when you answer my questions with just one or two words?"

I thought for a moment.

"No," I said.

19

Cooper grunted, and I smiled.

"Sorry," I said.

Cooper shook his head, and we walked on.

As we got closer I finally made out the form in front of our house. I smiled and cleared my throat.

"Your mule is back," I beckoned.

"What?" Cooper exclaimed, and Josie looked startled.

Jug-head stood in the middle of the street. He had a halter on, but the lead rope had been broken, and the rope was frayed and coming apart.

"What are you doing here?" Cooper frowned.

Soon as Jug-head heard Cooper's voice, he perked his ears and turned towards him.

"I believe that's the happiest I've ever seen that mule," I commented.

Cooper looked at me and scowled.

Chapter five

"He must've broke loose," Cooper commented as he walked up beside Jug-head and grabbed the lead rope. "I bet Jack is upset."

"Probably is," I agreed.

"What will we do?" Josie spoke up.

"I'll take him back in the morning," Cooper replied. "Tracks should be easy enough to follow."

"I'll go with you," I offered. "Give me something to do."

"You don't want to stay here and find out if you won?"

"Me being here won't change the results," I replied.

Cooper nodded thoughtfully, and he tugged on Jug-head's lead rope.

"I'll put him in a stall," Cooper said.

Josie nodded, and I asked, "Care for some coffee when you get back?"

"Sure."

"I'll make some," I said.

Cooper nodded as he led Jug-head down the street.

***

Cooper and I sat out on the front porch of our house. We drank coffee and enjoyed the cool night air. Josie was inside, getting ready for bed.

I told Cooper about Judge Parker's job offer. Afterwards, Cooper was silent as he thought on it.

"So I was right," Cooper finally said.

"You were," I nodded.

"If I wasn't married-," Cooper's voice trailed off.

"I know."

"However," Cooper continued. "I've also got to make a living. You lose that election, and I ain't got a job."

"If I do win," I said, "I could always resign and let you be sheriff."

"Sounds like you've already made up your mind," Cooper looked at me.

"I'm liking the thought of it," I admitted.

"And you expect me to stay here while you go get yourself killed?"

"Nobody's killed me yet," I replied. "And, like you said; you've got responsibilities now. I don't."

Cooper frowned thoughtfully.

"Well, I reckon we'll have to wait and see how the election ends up before we make any final decisions," Cooper said.

I nodded.

"And, whatever we decide, I'll have to talk it over with Josie first," Cooper said.

I nodded again, and it fell silent. A few minutes passed, and I cleared my throat.

"Our current living arrangement ain't too good for newlyweds," I said.

"It is what it is," Cooper shrugged.

"But you two don't have much alone time," I protested.

"We ain't complaining."

"You don't," I agreed. I hesitated, and suggested, "I could go for a ride every once in a while."

"What sort of ride?"

"You know. Ride around; see the country," I explained. "That would give you two some alone time."

Cooper frowned and looked thoughtful.

"I'll think on it," he said.

"Let me know," I said, and Cooper nodded.

Chapter six

Our house was small and simple. There was only one bedroom, a small front room, and a crowded kitchen. I slept on one side of the bedroom, and Josie and Cooper slept on the other side. There wasn't much privacy.

I woke early. I threw some wood in the wood stove, put on some coffee, and cooked a few eggs. We ate, and then Cooper and I went down to the livery stable and saddled our horses.

We mounted up and rode out into the street, with me leading Jug-head. We started to ride out, but then I spotted Jessica Tussle walking towards us.

Jessica was in her mid-twenties. She had a good figure, long blond hair, and light blue eyes.

For some reason, I always got a nervous feeling in the pit of my stomach whenever I was around her. And, I also could never think of anything to say.

Jessica smiled when she saw us, and I nodded back.

"Good morning, Yancy," she said.

"Jessica," I said.

"Going somewhere?"

"Yes."

Jessica paused, waiting for me to explain. A few awkward seconds passed before I realized that, and then Cooper stepped in and helped ease the tension.

"What brings you to town?" He asked pleasantly.

"We came for some supplies," Jessica explained, and then she looked at me. "Today's the big day."

"What do you mean?" I asked.

"You know. The election."

"Oh," I nodded. "That."

"Tussle is voting for you," Jessica said. "I made sure of that."

"I appreciate it."

Jessica nodded. Nobody could think of anything to say, and the silence was uncomfortable.

"Well," Jessica finally said. "Good luck with the election."

"I shouldn't need luck," I said abruptly, and I winced at how harsh that sounded.

"Well, good luck all the same," Jessica said, and she turned and walked up the street.

I watched her go, and then I glanced at Cooper. He sighed and shook his head.

"What?" I frowned.

"Oh, nothing," Cooper said, and we kicked up our horses and headed out.

Chapter seven

We rode out of town a ways, and then Cooper started hunting for the wagon tracks. Coop had once been one of the best trackers in the Union army, so it didn't take him long to find them.

The country around Midway was mainly flat, with a few rolling hills. The grass was tall, and there was a little brush, but not much.

Cooper led the way, and I rode beside him, leading Jug-head. We tried to trot, but Jug-head wouldn't cooperate. So we slowed to a walk, and our horses couldn't help but nip at the green grass.

It was silent, but then I heard Cooper sigh. I looked at him and frowned.

"What is it?" I demanded to know.

"It's painful," Cooper declared.

"What is?" I frowned, confused.

"You and Jessica," Cooper explained. "Mostly, you're always calm and collected. But whenever you're around her, you get all tight and tense. So does she. Watching you two try to have a conversation is painful to watch."

I scowled, but didn't reply.

"You both like each other," Cooper continued. "Anybody can see that. What's the problem?"

"You really want to know?"

"I want to know."

I sighed and collected my thoughts.

"When I settle down, I want to take care of somebody," I said.

"I feel the same way about Josie," Cooper nodded.

"But Jessica doesn't need taking care of," I replied. "She's already got more money than I'll ever make."

Cooper looked at me and frowned.

"Is that the only thing holding you back?"

"No," I replied. "There's more."

"Such as?"

"Lee Mattingly," I declared.

"What about him?"

"He likes her, and I think she likes him," I said. "And, we both know that Jessica was somehow involved with Stew Baine escaping from jail."

"Is that still bothering you?"

"Yes," I said.

"Stew Baine's dead, Yancy. Does all that really matter now?"

"It does to me," I replied.

"Yancy, you can't always have things your way," Cooper reasoned. "Sometimes, you've got to adjust to make things work. And, I wouldn't worry about her having all that money. It ain't her fault."

"It's just the principal of it," I argued. "A man is supposed to take care of his wife, not the other way around."

Cooper sighed.

"I wish Josie and I had that problem," he said wistfully. "I'm pretty sure we could overcome it."

"Mebbe I'm just not the marrying sort," I said.

"You want to be alone all your life?"

"I ain't alone," I objected. "I've got you and Josie."

Cooper frowned, but didn't reply.

Chapter eight

"They made it further than I figured they would," Cooper commented as we searched the country in front of us. "I don't see any sign of them."

It was nearing midday. It was getting hot, and sweat streaked down our faces.

"Are they getting any fresher?" I beckoned at the tracks.

"Some," Cooper nodded.

I had always marveled at how Cooper could follow and read sign. To me it looked like scratches in the ground, but to Cooper it was like a map.

"We should have packed something to eat," I said wistfully.

"I've got some *chigustei,*" Cooper offered.

"Some what?"

"That's what Josie calls it," Cooper explained. "It's Injun food. She made me some. Says it's good for me."

"What is it?"

"Not sure," Cooper replied. "I think it's made out of corn."

"Any good?"

"Ain't tried it yet."

"Well, I reckon it's all we have," I said, and Cooper nodded.

There was a tree up ahead. We rode over to it, dismounted, and picketed our horses. I grabbed our canteens while Cooper dug out the *chigustei* from his saddlebags, and we sat under the shade of the tree.

Cooper unwrapped the food and handed it to me.

Chigustei sort of resembled a Mexican-style tortilla, only a lot thicker. I frowned as I studied it, and I took a small bite. I swallowed and took a larger bite.

"How is it?" Cooper asked.

"Dry," I said as I took a swig from my canteen.

Cooper took a cautious bite. His face was thoughtful as he chewed and swallowed.

"It ain't that bad," he said.

"Be better with some coffee," I said.

It fell silent as we ate. I finally choked down my *chigustei,* and Cooper offered me another one.

"No thanks," I said.

"Did you like it?"

"I like steak and beans better," I said.

Cooper nodded. He took a swig from his canteen and looked at me.

"There's something I've been meaning to talk with you about," he said.

"What is it?"

"It's Josie," Cooper said. "I'm not sure if you've noticed, but it's been hard on her, living around white folks again."

"After all she's been through, I'd say that's to be expected," I replied.

"She feels out of place," Cooper said, and added, "You know she doesn't like to talk much."

"That's what I like best about her."

Cooper frowned at me, and continued, "She also doesn't like how the other women folk talk about her and stare at her."

"Tell her to stare back."

"But that ain't all," Cooper said. "Josie was married to an Injun, and they don't like that either."

"That wasn't Josie's fault," I replied. "She had no say in the matter."

"The town folks don't see it that way."

I thought on that and grunted.

"Well, who cares what they think."

"Josie does," Cooper said, and added, "And another thing; Josie feels like she's a burden to us. She wants to start helping out."

"Doing what?"

"Doing the dishes, laundry; things like that."

"Long as it makes her feel better, I have no problem with that," I smiled.

"She also wants to cook for us."

"Can she cook?" I frowned.

"Some."

"And what will she be cooking?" I asked suspiciously.

"She learned a lot while living with the Indians," Cooper replied innocently.

"But I'm not an Injun," I objected. "I like steak and beans, not plants and *chigustei*."

Cooper looked at me and frowned.

"We're going to eat whatever she cooks, and we're also going to like it. We're trying to build her confidence, you understand?"

"She ain't my wife," I protested. "Why do I have to suffer?"

Cooper scowled. I sighed, and then nodded.

"Fine," I muttered. "Long as I have my coffee, I reckon I can eat just about anything."

"Good," Cooper nodded and stood. "Well, we'd best be going."

"We wouldn't want to miss supper," I commented wryly as I followed after him.

Chapter nine

We pushed on. I led Jug-head while Cooper followed the tracks.

A half hour passed, and Cooper suddenly pulled up. He leaned low out of the saddle as he looked down.

"What is it?" I asked as I stopped beside him.

"See those horse tracks?" He pointed.

I looked and nodded.

"They ain't shod," Cooper said.

"Injuns?"

"Probably," Cooper nodded.

Cooper dismounted, walked forward a little, and squatted on his heels.

"They're following the wagon," he finally said.

"How many?"

"Hard to say. Ten, mebbe twelve."

"They might just be curious," I said hopefully.

"I don't think so," Cooper disagreed as he climbed back into the saddle.

"How old are the tracks?" I asked.

"I'd say last night, or this morning."

"And how far ahead is wagon?"

"Tracks are too mingled to tell," Cooper said.

I frowned as I thought on that.

"Well, things just got a bit more interesting," I finally said.

"I'd say so," Cooper nodded.

***

We checked our weapons and rode on. We had Henry rifles in our scabbards, and we both wore Colts.

I was better with my Colt, but Cooper preferred his Henry. He had a special way of swinging it up, and he was almost as fast as I was with a Colt.

We rode slow, with Cooper hanging out of the saddle, studying the tracks. I followed and watched the surrounding landscape for anything suspicious.

Another half hour passed, and I spotted a dark object a long ways out in front of us.

"Look," I beckoned.

Cooper pulled himself back into the saddle and squinted ahead.

"Looks like the wagon," Cooper said.

"I don't see any Injuns," I commented.

Cooper turned in his saddle, dug in his saddlebags, and pulled out a spyglass. He squinted through it, and his face turned grim.

"It's the wagon," Cooper confirmed. "Somebody's stretched out on the ground. I don't see anybody else."

"Is it a 'he' or 'she'?"

"Looks like a 'he'."

"Dead?"

"He ain't moving."

"Well," I said. "Let's go find out."

Chapter ten

Cooper pulled out his Henry and held it ready while I grabbed my Colt.

We kicked up our horses, and we were real watchful as we rode on.

We stopped in front of the wagon. I searched the surrounding landscape once more, and then I looked around.

The wagon had been looted, and there were pots and pans scattered all about. There was also a dead mule beside the wagon with several arrows in him.

There were the remains of a small campfire, and a coffee pot had also been knocked over.

A tall, slender man was lying facedown on the ground. His hand and sleeve were in the campfire, and his hand and arm had been badly burned. He had also been scalped. He had three arrows in him, and he was dead.

"Is that Jack?" I asked.

"That's him," Cooper nodded.

We dismounted. We tied our horses to some nearby bushes, and then we looked around some more.

"There was a woman and a boy," Cooper told me.

"They might have been taken," I suggested.

Cooper nodded, and he walked around the wagon while I studied the campfire. I felt the coals, and they were cold.

"Yancy," Cooper's voice was sharp.

I hurried around the wagon.

Mrs. Walden was lying on her back, near the wagon wheel. She had been scalped. An arrow was in her shoulder, and another one was in her stomach. Cooper had knelt beside her, and he was checking for a pulse.

"She's alive," Cooper said.

Suddenly, Mrs. Walden opened her eyes. She was startled, and she looked up at Cooper through terrified eyes.

"Take it easy, ma'am," Cooper said gently. "It's me, Cooper Landon. We met yesterday at Midway."

She stared at him for several seconds. She blinked, and then nodded.

"Jack," she said in a whisper.

"He's dead, ma'am."

"My boy, Wyatt."

"We haven't found him yet," Cooper said.

"They took him," she stammered. "I saw it. The big one. He took Wyatt."

Cooper glanced at me and looked back at Mrs. Walden.

"The big one. He took Wyatt," Mrs. Walden said again. "Please, *please*, get Wyatt back."

"You rest easy now," Cooper said. "We'll find him."

Mrs. Walden managed to nod, and Cooper stood and looked at me with a grim expression.

"I'll walk out a ways and look the tracks over," Cooper said.

I nodded. I looked at Mrs. Walden once more, and then I grabbed a shovel from the wagon.

Chapter eleven

Cooper and I had been around death for many years. We both knew there was no use trying to move Mrs. Walden.

While Cooper studied the tracks, I dug a grave for Jack. By the time I finished, Mrs. Walden was gone. Cooper returned, and he helped me dig another grave.

It took us an hour to get them buried. Afterwards, we sat in the shade of the wagon and sipped water from our canteens.

"Which way are they headed?" I asked.

"Northwest."

"Any chance we could overtake them?"

Cooper shook his head.

"Don't think so. Tracks are at least ten, twelve hours old."

"So a horse race is out of the question."

"Yep. It's going to be a long ride and take a lot of time to catch them."

"Well," I said thoughtfully. "Long rides go better when you're prepared. Reckon we'll go back to Midway and get prepared."

Cooper shot me a surprised look.

"You're coming with me?"

"You told Mrs. Walden we'd go after Wyatt."

"I did, but you didn't," Cooper replied. "What about the election?"

I grunted in response, and asked, "Where do you reckon they're headed?"

"I'd say Valverde's Pass."

"From there, they'll go up into the mountains," I figured.

"Yep."

I sighed.

"They won't be easy to find in those mountains," I said.

"Josie will probably want to come along," Cooper said thoughtfully. "She knows those mountains."

"That could be helpful," I said.

"Sure could."

I nodded and stood.

"Well, we'd best be going," I suggested.

Cooper followed me to our horses. We untied them, climbed into the saddle, and rode back east. This time, Cooper led the mule.

I glanced at Jug-head while we rode along.

"Looks like you got your mule back," I said solemnly.

Cooper didn't reply. Instead, he just grunted.

Chapter twelve

Darkness overtook us when we were about halfway back to Midway. But we knew the country, so we weren't worried.

"Mrs. Walden said that a big Injun took Wyatt," Cooper recalled while we rode along.

"Most Apaches are small," I replied.

"No Worries isn't."

"No, he ain't," I said thoughtfully. "He's about the same size as you."

"Reckon he's the one who took Wyatt?"

"Could be," I said thoughtfully.

We'd had dealings with No Worries before. He was a young war chief of the Apaches, and he led his growing band with a ruthless recklessness. His name was becoming a household name, right up there with Geronimo.

"If it is him, they'll probably go to their summer camp up in the mountains," Cooper figured. "Josie knows where it is. She told me about it."

"That would be a good place to start," I said.

"It would be better if we had something to trade," Cooper suggested.

"You think No Worries would trade with us?"

"Josie will know."

"We could trade Jug-head," I suggested wryly, and Cooper smiled.

We rode a bit further, and I glanced at Cooper.

"No Worries would recognize me and Josie."

"That could be a problem."

"But, he might not remember you," I reasoned.

"Handsome as I am, would be hard to forget," Cooper smiled wryly.

"But you were wounded and looked awful," I reminded. "And, No Worries was focused on counting coup against me. He probably didn't even notice you."

"So I get to ride in alone?"

"No," I frowned. "We'll bring someone else along."

"Who?"

"Don't know yet."

"And we'll also need trade goods," Cooper reminded.

"We'll think of something."

Cooper smiled faintly, and it fell silent.

"I wonder who won the election," Cooper said after a while.

This time, it was me that grunted in response.

Chapter thirteen

It was late by the time we got back. However, there were lights lit up and down the street, and the town was crowded and full of excitement.

I spotted Judge Parker sitting on the porch at the jail, so we rode over to him. I also spotted Josie, walking up from our house.

"Well, look who finally showed up," Judge Parker said.

I was about to reply when we heard a commotion behind us. We turned in the saddle and looked.

Jason Wagons was walking towards us, and a huge crowd followed. As he got closer, I saw that there was a sheriff's badge pinned on his vest's pocket.

"I don't believe it," I heard Cooper say softly.

Wagons looked boastful as he stopped in front of us. Just like that, it got quiet and still.

"Well, I won," Wagons beamed.

"I see that," I said, and my face was emotionless. "Congratulations."

"I won in a landslide," Wagons couldn't help but add. "You did get a few votes, though."

I didn't have an answer for that, so I was silent.

"Everybody's been wondering where you've been all day," Wagons continued.

"We ran into trouble."

"Oh?" Wagons looked interested. "Anything I need to know about?"

I ignored Wagons and looked at Judge Parker.

"A wagon was attacked by Injuns, about a half day's ride from here. They killed a man and his wife and took their boy."

A nervous murmur went through the crowd, and Wagons got all excited looking.

"This is sheriff's business," he declared. "You should have told me right away."

"There's nothing you can do about it, Wagons," I said sourly.

"We can go after them," Wagons replied, and several men in the crowd voiced their support. "I'll raise a posse."

I sighed and looked at Cooper, and he cleared his throat.

"They're too far ahead," he said. "You'd never catch them."

"But we can try," Wagons protested.

"Look. A white man will ride a horse until he's tired, but then an Injun will come along and ride that horse another thirty miles, and then eat him," Cooper explained patiently.

"Well, we've got to do something," Wagons insisted.

"Yancy and I have already decided," Cooper said. "We're going after them, but it's going to take time."

"You ain't going without me," Wagons declared.

"A sheriff needs to stay in his town," I spoke up.

Wagons turned and glared at me.

"I don't take orders from you anymore, Yancy. You need to remember that."

I ignored Wagons and looked at Judge Parker.

"Judge," I said, "If I were a Texas Ranger, would I have authority over a local sheriff?"

"Of course," Judge Parker nodded.

"Swear me in."

Chapter fourteen

"Now hold on," Wagons started to protest.

"Sheriff Wagons," Judge Parker interrupted.

"Yes?" Wagons looked at him.

"You are interfering with official business. As a Judge, I'm ordering you to drop this. Yancy and Cooper will take care of it."

"You want to do something," I added, "You can ride out tomorrow and get the Walden's wagon."

Wagons didn't like it. His face was sullen as he turned and walked off, and his movements were jerky and abrupt.

"The rest of you break up and go home," Judge Parker spoke to the crowd.

There were a few mumblings, but the crowd moved on down the street.

Soon as they were gone, Josie walked up beside Cooper's horse. She smiled at Cooper, and he returned the smile with one of his own.

"You were gone, long time," Josie said.

"We didn't mean to be," Cooper said, and added, "Did you hear everything?"

Josie nodded.

"We're getting that boy back," Cooper declared.

"I go with you?" Josie's face looked hopeful.

"Of course," Cooper agreed. "We need you. Ain't that right, Yancy?"

"You know those mountains better than we do," I said.

Josie looked pleased, and she smiled.

"How are you planning on getting that boy back?" Judge Parker asked from the porch.

"Be more peaceful if we could trade for him," Cooper replied, and he looked at Josie and asked, "Would that be possible, Josie?"

"Have to be a good trade," Josie replied.

Cooper and I looked at each other and frowned.

"Do you have any trade goods?" Judge Parker asked.

"We've got this mule," I beckoned.

Judge Parker smiled and stood.

"I have a thought," he said. "Care to join me for supper?"

"I could sure eat," I replied.

"I'll meet you boys at the café then," Judge Parker said.

I nodded, but Josie spoke before I could reply.

"I cooked supper. It is on the stove."

"What?" I looked at her.

"There is plenty," Josie said.

"What is it?" I narrowed my eyes.

"Indian stew."

I looked at Cooper and frowned, but he ignored me.

"That sounds wonderful," Cooper said, and he looked at Judge Parker. "Care to join us, Judge?"

Judge Parker agreed, and they walked towards our house.

I frowned thoughtfully and followed after them.

Chapter fifteen

Our front room was small, and our table filled the room. We squeezed into a chair, and Josie hustled about.

"I made coffee," she said, and she poured us all a cup. She also handed me the sugar bowl.

I poured in my normal three spoonfuls, stirred, and took a swig.

The coffee had a burnt taste to it. I swallowed and coughed and reached for the sugar bowl.

Judge Parker took a swig, and his face was emotionless. I offered him the sugar bowl, and he didn't say a word as he poured some in.

Josie looked excited as she served us. She placed a bowl of stew in front of us, and I frowned as I studied it.

I picked up my spoon and sampled it. It was bad. I couldn't help but make a face as I swallowed.

I glanced at Cooper and Judge Parker. Cooper showed no emotion, and Judge Parker looked thoughtful as they swallowed.

"How is it?" Josie asked anxiously.

"Fine, just fine," Cooper said, and Judge Parker and I mumbled something and forced smiles.

Josie looked pleased, and we returned to our stew.

It was quiet and sober while we ate.

Judge Parker's bowl was halfway empty when he finally pushed his bowl back. I did the same and looked at Cooper. He was still eating, and I could tell by the look on his face that he was determined to finish it.

"Thanks for supper, ma'am," Judge Parker said.

"More?"

"No, thank you."

"Coffee?"

"I'm good. Thank you, ma'am."

Josie smiled and grabbed our bowls. She carried them into the kitchen, and when she returned she sat beside Cooper.

"I know somebody who has trade goods," Judge Parker announced.

"Who?" I asked.

"Ike Nash."

Cooper and I glanced at each other, and I frowned.

"I don't follow," I admitted.

Judge Parker leaned forward in his chair.

"I told you Ike has a new partner. His name is Morgan Gant. His brother, Boyle, rides with him."

"I've heard of 'em," I said thoughtfully.

"They do gun work?" Cooper asked me.

"Yep."

"They good as us?"

"They ain't any worse."

Cooper frowned thoughtfully while Josie looked worried.

"They're bad men," Judge Parker said. "Bank robberies, rustling, killing; they've done it all. Morgan is the interesting one."

"How so?" I asked.

"From what I hear, he's very sophisticated. He even went to West Point before the war."

"One of them educated fellers," I said.

"Yes, very much so."

"And now he's trading rifles to the Injuns," I said.

"Yes, and Ike is supplying the rifles."

"What do you have in mind?" I asked.

"In six days, Ike is sending a man to Bronc, New Mexico, with two mules, packed with rifles. Morgan and Boyle are supposed to meet him there and pick up the rifles."

"And then they'll go up into the mountains and trade with the Injuns," I reasoned.

"That is correct."

"Have Morgan and Boyle already made contact with the Injuns?"

"My source didn't know," Judge Parker said.

"So where do we come in?" Cooper spoke up.

"I want you two to pose as Morgan and Boyle," Judge Parker announced. "Meet Ike's man in Bronc, pick up the rifles, and go get that boy back."

"What about Ike's man?" I asked.

"Leave him alone for now," Judge Parker said. "We'll get him next time."

"Next time?"

"Once the routine starts, they're supposed to meet every eight weeks," Judge Parker explained.

"A steady supply," I said.

Judge Parker nodded.

"What about the real Morgan and Boyle?" Cooper spoke up. "We can't all be showing up at Bronc at the same time."

"Last I heard, Morgan and Boyle were at Landry," Judge Parker said.

"We know the town," I said.

"I want you and Cooper to go up there and kill them," Judger Parker announced abruptly.

Cooper and I were startled.

"Kill them?" Cooper asked distastefully.

"There can't be two sets of Gant brothers running around," Judge Parked replied.

"What if they surrender?" Cooper asked.

"I can't send them to prison," Judge Parker said. "Ike would find out."

Cooper looked at me and frowned.

"Look, these are bad men," Judge Parker explained patiently. "I don't care how you do it. Just get rid of them."

Cooper and I nodded soberly.

"Are you sure you want to put rifles in the hands of Injuns?" I asked.

"Course not," Judge Parker said. "Disable them first."

"They already fell for that once," Cooper warned. "I doubt they'd fall for it again."

"Don't disable them all," Judge Parker suggested. "And, make sure the ones they try aren't disabled."

Cooper and I smiled faintly.

"You make it sound so easy," I said.

Judge Parker smiled and shrugged.

"There's another problem," I announced.

"What's that?"

"It'll probably be No Worries we're dealing with. He would recognize me and Josie," I explained.

"And I don't speak Apache," Cooper added.

"Do you know anybody else that does?" Judge Parker asked.

"Yes," I said suddenly. "I do. He lives in Landry."

"Who is it?" Cooper looked at me.

"Kolorado."

"Him? He'd never agree to go with us," Cooper objected.

"He might, under the right circumstances," I said thoughtfully, and I glanced at Judge Parker. "Judge, I need you to write up a pardon."

"For who?"

"Kolorado."

"Who exactly is Kolorado?" Judge Parker asked.

"He's an old-timer who owns a livery stable," I said, and added, "But, Kolorado isn't his real name. He had to change it."

"Why?"

"I have no idea."

"So why the pardon?"

"For leverage," I explained.

Judge Parker frowned, and then he nodded.

"All right. I'll have it for you in the morning."

I nodded, and it fell silent as we thought on things.

"So, we have to go to Landry and kill Morgan and Boyle, recruit Kolorado, go to Bronc, meet Ike's man and get the rifles, and then go up into the mountains and trade for the boy with disabled rifles," Cooper surmised.

"Sounds about right," I said.

"And you only have six days," Judge Parker reminded.

"We like a good challenge," I smiled.

Chapter sixteen

Judge Parker swore us in as Texas Rangers the next
morning.

"Here's your badges," he said as he handed them over.

We were at the jail, and the only witnesses were Josie
and Sheriff Wagons. Wagons sat behind his desk, and he
still looked sullen.

"Remember," Judge Parker warned, "Keep those badges
hidden when you boys are doing your Pinkerton work."

"Pinkerton work?" Wagons asked.

"Forget you heard that," Judge Parker frowned at him.

"Yes, sir."

Judge Parked turned back to me.

"Here's the pardon," he handed it over.

I put the pardon and my badge in my pocket, and then I
shook Judge Parker's hand.

"Good luck," Judge Parker said.

I nodded and looked at Wagons.

"Wagons," I said dryly.

Wagons nodded sullenly.

I looked around the jail once more, and then I walked
out the door. Cooper and Josie followed.

***

It took us an hour to get everything gathered up. We
grabbed enough provisions to last a couple of weeks, and
we packed Jug-head down with the supplies. We also
packed an extra pair of clothes for each of us.

Josie looked different this morning. She wore a man's
shirt and buckskin pants, and she also wore moccasins that
came all the way up to her knees. To me, she seemed more
comfortable dressed this way.

Josie also had a bow and some arrows that she packed on Jug-head, and I frowned curiously.

"Are you any good with that?" I asked.

"Yes."

I looked at Cooper, and he nodded.

"She can hit what she aims at," he confirmed.

"Might come in handy," I said.

"Sure might," Cooper agreed.

"Well, let's go saddle the horses," I suggested.

We were almost done when the stagecoach pulled into the street. Passengers that were waiting threw their luggage on top and climbed in.

We led our horses out into the street, and I spotted J.T. Tussle and Jessica walking towards the stage.

Jessica saw me, and she said something to Tussle and walked over. As she got closer, that tight feeling returned to my stomach.

"Good morning, Yancy," she said.

"Jessica," I nodded.

She nodded back, and then we looked at each other.

"I'm sorry you lost the election," she finally said.

"It wasn't meant to be," I shrugged.

"Are you going somewhere?"

"Yes."

She paused, waiting for me to explain, but I wasn't sure if I should.

I spotted Tussle throwing luggage on top of the stage.

"How 'bout you?" I asked instead. "Where are you and Tussle headed?"

"Empty-lake," Jessica said. "J.T. has some business there, and I wanted to go along."

"Lee Mattingly is in Empty-lake," I said thoughtfully.

"He sure is," Jessica said, and she looked excited. "I need to see him too."

I frowned at that.

"Have a good trip," I said abruptly.

Jessica looked at me and smiled, but I didn't acknowledge it.

"Well, goodbye, Yancy."

"Bye."

Jessica hesitated, but then she turned and walked over to the stage. I watched her climb in, and then I looked at Cooper. He was smiling, and I scowled.

"Like I said," Cooper said. "Painful. Just painful."

"She *needs* to see Lee? What does that mean?" I asked as I ignored Cooper's comment.

"I don't know, Yancy," Cooper replied, and suggested, "Mebbe it came out wrong. Probably meant 'hope'."

I thought on that for a moment.

"'I *hope* to see Lee' ain't any better," I complained.

"I'm not sure what you want me to say, Yancy," Cooper said.

"It's not what you're saying, it's what she said," I said in disgust.

Cooper didn't reply.

"She ain't never *needed* to see me," I muttered.

Cooper nodded politely, and I sighed as I climbed on my horse.

"I'm tired of this town," I said. "You ready?"

Cooper looked at Josie, and she nodded.

"We're ready," Cooper said.

"Then let's go," I said, and we kicked up our horses.

Chapter seventeen

We traveled in silence. Cooper led the way, and Josie followed him. I led Jug-head and brought up the rear.

Cooper and I developed a routine during the war whenever we traveled. Since he was the better tracker, he always led while I searched the landscape, looking for anything suspicious. And, even when we weren't tracking something, we always stuck to the same routine.

It was a two-day ride to Landry. We had made the ride many times, and we knew the way. There was a mesa halfway between Midway and Landry, and the plan was to camp there.

It was midmorning when Cooper glanced back at me.

"I'm curious," he said.

"About what?"

"What bothers you more," Cooper explained. "Losing the election, or Jessica?"

"Do I have to pick?"

Cooper grinned and turned back around in the saddle while I scowled at him.

The day passed smoothly. The country was open with rolling hills, and we made good time. As it was getting dark, we arrived at the base of the mesa.

"I'll make some coffee," I said as we dismounted.

"I'll do it," Josie offered.

"Don't worry about it," I replied abruptly.

Josie frowned, but she didn't say anything.

Before she could change her mind, I gathered some wood and built a fire. Meanwhile, Cooper brought me the coffee pot while Josie tended to the horses.

I glanced at Cooper after the coffee was on.

"I'm about to starve, Coop," I said in a quiet voice. "I haven't had a decent meal in two days."

"I know. Me too," Cooper admitted.

50

"I could cook something," I suggested.

"No. Josie wants to."

I scowled.

"That was the worst stew I've ever attempted to eat," I declared.

"It was bad," Cooper agreed.

Suddenly, we heard an angry gasp behind us. We spun around, and Josie stood behind us.

"Boy, you're quiet," I said.

"Josie," Cooper stood.

Anger flashed in Josie's eyes. She shook her head and stormed off.

Cooper looked at me and frowned, and then he hurried after her.

"Josie. Wait!"

Josie kept walking, but Cooper finally caught her. He reached for her shoulder, but she shrugged him off and kept walking.

They disappeared into the darkness. I tried not to listen, but I couldn't help but hear sharp, abrupt words from Josie. I wasn't sure, but it sounded like she was talking in Apache.

A few minutes passed, and Cooper walked back up to the fire. He had a pained expression on his face. His shoulders were hunched, and he had the tips of his fingers in his pockets.

"Coffee?" I asked.

Cooper nodded. I jumped to my feet, poured him a cup, and handed it to him.

It was silent as we drank our coffee. Cooper just stared into the fire, and I frowned as I watched him.

"She mad?" I finally asked.

Cooper took a swig of coffee.

"Remember those rides you were offering to take?" He asked.

"Sure," I nodded.

"There's no need for 'em right now."
I tried not to smile.
"I'm sorry, Coop," I said as earnestly as I could.
"So am I," Cooper said.

Chapter eighteen

I took advantage of the situation and cooked supper. I had brought some salt pork, and I placed thick slices in my frying pan. It wasn't long until the pork was hissing, and my stomach growled.

When the salt pork was done, I warmed up some cold biscuits that I had. Next, I made a plate for Cooper and handed it to him, and then I fixed my own plate.

"What about Josie?" I asked.

"I'd leave her alone for now."

"She's your wife," I replied, and it fell silent as we ate.

I tore into my salt pork with a vengeance. It tasted good, and I washed it down with several cups of coffee.

"Was Josie speaking Apache?" I asked.

"She does that when she's upset."

"Well, least you don't understand what she's saying," I tried to be helpful.

"I may not understand the words, but I still get the gist."

"Yeah," I said thoughtfully. "I think I got the gist too." Cooper nodded solemnly.

"I'm sorry, Coop," I said. "I should have kept quiet."

"She'll get over it."

"You can blame me if you want," I offered.

"Thanks," Cooper said. "I will."

I looked at Cooper and smiled, but he didn't return the smile.

"I reckon she had to know, sooner or later," Cooper said. "I just wish I could have broke it to her a bit more gentle-like."

"I don't think being a cook is her calling in life," I suggested. "She seems more comfortable out here, away from town."

"It's what she's used to."

"It's what I'm used to also," I said as I reached for the coffee pot. "More coffee?"

Cooper nodded, and I poured us both another cup. It was silent for a bit, and Cooper glanced at me.

"Does this business with Morgan and Boyle bother you any?"

"What about it?"

"We've killed lots of men before," Cooper said. "But, never quite like this."

"What's the difference?"

"Everybody else got a chance to surrender," Cooper explained.

"I reckon they did," I said.

"But Morgan and Boyle won't have that option."

"No, they won't," I agreed.

"And that doesn't bother you?"

"It does some," I admitted.

"I can't stop thinking about it."

"What's the penalty for murder?" I asked.

"Death by hanging," Cooper said.

"Well, you heard what Judge Parker said," I reasoned. "These men are killers. How I see it is that Judge Parker sentenced them, and now we're carrying that order out, just like any hangman would."

Cooper scratched his jaw thoughtfully.

"I reckon that's one way to look at it," he finally said.

I nodded.

"Course, they could kill us first," Cooper reckoned.

"Could happen."

"So, they'll either kill us, or we'll kill them," Cooper figured.

"That would be correct."

"And the first ones that die," Cooper declared, "loses."

I smiled and nodded.

Chapter nineteen

Josie was so quiet, I didn't even notice when she came back.

Cooper and I drank a few more cups of coffee, and I suddenly spotted Josie, sitting beside the fire. I was startled, and I dropped my cup of coffee.

"Boy, you're quiet," I said again.

Josie looked at me, and her face was emotionless. I smiled, but she didn't acknowledge it.

The night air was cool. Cooper stood, grabbed a blanket, and offered it to her. She shook her head abruptly. Cooper frowned at her, and then he sat back down.

Meanwhile, I made her a plate and held it out to her.

"Hungry?" I asked.

She stared at it. She hesitated, but then she grabbed it. I smiled and poured her a cup of coffee.

It was silent while Josie ate. I looked at Cooper, but he just shrugged.

"Well, we should be at Landry tomorrow evening," I said, just to be saying something.

Neither Josie nor Cooper replied.

"Things might get busy then," I said.

Again, it was silent.

A few more awkward minutes passed. Josie finished her supper, and then we just sat there.

"Well, think I'll turn in," I finally said.

Cooper nodded. I grabbed my bedroll, walked away from the fire a ways, and bedded down.

***

Josie didn't offer to cook breakfast the next morning, so I did.

Nobody talked while we ate. Josie looked sullen, and Cooper looked irritable.

We packed up camp after breakfast, and we saddled our horses and rode out.

It took us several hours to climb the mesa. It was a steep climb, and we had to ride back and forth instead of straight up.

Soon as we reached the top, Cooper took the lead. I followed with Jug-head, and Josie followed me.

It was an uneventful day. Josie never said a word, and Cooper didn't say much either. Occasionally I would see them looking at each other, but that was all.

We arrived at Landry about an hour before dark.

Landry was one of those towns that existed mainly for folks passing through. There was only one main street, and it always seemed to be soggy and muddy. There was also a stink that sort of rose up from the ground, and everything had a greasy look about it.

This was the place where Cooper, Rondo, and I had killed Wade Davis and his sons. Cooper had been shot in the hip again, and I'd been hit in the shoulder. This was also the town where Cooper and Josie had met.

"Lotta memories here," Cooper commented.

"Yeah. Painful ones," I said, and I reached up and patted my shoulder.

"Not all of them," Cooper said, and he looked at Josie.

They stared at each other, and Cooper smiled. Josie started to frown, but then she smiled back.

"Well, let's go see Kolorado," I suggested.

Cooper nodded, and we rode on down the street to Kolorado's livery stable.

Kolorado was sitting on his bench out in front. He was chewing tobacco, and between spits he was whittling on a stick.

He wore the same sweat stained shirt. And, even though it was warm, he also wore white long johns underneath, and

56

the sleeves and collar had a salty, brown look. He also had a stringy, white moustache that was stained by tobacco juice.

Kolorado looked up and spotted us. First, he stared at Josie, and then he looked at me and Cooper.

"Well, I see you ain't been killed yet," He grunted.

"It's good to see you too," I said.

"What are you doing here this time?"

"We rode all this way just to see you," I forced a smile. Kolorado grunted.

"Sure you did. I reckon you'll be wanting to stay here tonight."

"Thanks for the invite," I said.

"It ain't no invite," he scowled. "You'll pay, or you can go on down the street."

I smiled and nodded.

"I don't understand why you Landons always want to stay here anyway," Kolorado muttered as he stood. "Hotel would be more comfortable."

"We like it here," I said, and added, "Besides, we've always paid."

"You have," Kolorado agreed, and then he sighed. "Well, come on. Let's get you settled."

We dismounted and followed Kolorado inside, and we unsaddled our horses and fed them hay. While we worked, Kolorado leaned against a stall and stared at Josie.

"I see you're still with Cooper," Kolorado said.

"Yes," Josie nodded.

"Speaking English again too?"

"Some."

Kolorado nodded and looked at Jug-head.

"I see you still have that mule."

"I can't seem to get rid of him," Cooper spoke up.

"Why do you want to get rid of him? He's a good mule."

"You want to buy him back?" Cooper asked hopefully.

57

"No," Kolorado replied, and asked, "Where's Lee? Is he riding with you?"

"He is not," I replied abruptly.

"I always liked Lee."

"I don't," I said, and then I changed the subject. "Kolorado, I've been looking for a feller like you. Buy you supper?"

Kolorado's face brightened.

"Well! I've been looking for a feller like you too. Let's go."

Kolorado walked out of the livery. I looked at Cooper, and he smiled and shrugged. I frowned back, and we followed after Kolorado.

Chapter twenty

There was only one café in town.

The café reminded me some of the café back at Midway.
The place was dirty and grimy, and there were only two
options on the menu. Mystery stew, or fried salt pork. We
all chose mystery stew, and we washed it down with plenty
of coffee.

Soon as Kolorado's stew was gone, he took a deep swig
of coffee and pushed his bowl back.

"Thanks for supper," Kolorado said, and he stood and
grabbed his hat.

"Hold on," I said.

"What for?" Kolorado scowled.

I reached into my pocket, pulled out my Texas Rangers
badge, pinned it on my vest, and gave it a little pat.

"We've got important business to discuss," I said.

Kolorado narrowed his eyes as he studied my badge.

"You're a Texas Ranger now?"

"I am."

"Why didn't you tell me?" He demanded to know.

"I thought I just did," I frowned.

"What do you want with me?"

"Sit down, and I'll tell you," I said.

Kolorado's scowl remained. He studied us for a
moment, and he eased back into his chair.

"I ain't got much time, so be quick about it," he said.

"More coffee?"

"No."

I nodded. I refilled my cup, poured some sugar in, and
stirred. Kolorado watched me with a scowl.

"Let's start with Morgan and Boyle Gant," I said.

"What about 'em?"

"You know them?"

"I know who they are."

I glanced at Cooper and nodded. Meanwhile, Josie watched us with wide eyes.

"They live here," I said.

"Most of the time," Kolorado agreed.

"Are they here now?"

"No," Kolorado said, and Cooper and I looked up sharply.

"Oh? Where are they?" I asked.

"How should I know?"

I frowned.

"When did they leave?"

"They rode out this morning," Kolorado said, and added, "They had a pack mule too."

"That'll slow them down some," Cooper spoke up.

I nodded, and Kolorado studied us curiously.

"You're going after Morgan and Boyle?"

"We are," I nodded.

"Why?"

"That's Texas Ranger business," I said.

"Can I leave now?"

"No," I said, and Kolorado scowled again.

It was silent while I collected my thoughts. I reached into my pocket, pulled out the pardon, and set it on the table. Kolorado glanced at it and looked back at me.

"Kolorado," I said in a clear, stern voice.

"Yes?"

"I know why you had to change your name."

Cooper shot me a startled look, but I ignored him.

"How did you figure that out?" Kolorado narrowed his eyes.

"I'm a Texas Ranger," I reminded. "I know things."

It fell silent as Kolorado thought on that, and I waited patiently.

"I like you boys," Kolorado finally said. "But, I'll die fighting before I go back to prison."

This time, it was me and Cooper that were startled. However, I managed to conceal my surprise. I glanced at Cooper and looked back at Kolorado.

"Mebbe it won't come to that," I said.

"How's that?"

I explained about the Waldens, and about how Wyatt had been captured by the Indians. Afterwards, Kolorado frowned thoughtfully.

"Why tell me all of this?"

"We're getting Wyatt back," I said.

"So?"

"We'll need help," I said, and added, "Your help."

"How?"

"You speak Apache. We don't."

"But she does," Kolorado pointed at Josie.

"No Worries would recognize her."

"What does No Worries have to do with this?"

"That's probably who we'll be dealing with," I explained, and asked curiously, "Do you know No Worries?"

"Sure."

"How do you know him? Have you traded with him before?"

Kolorado frowned and looked at me suspiciously.

"I thought you knew why I had to change my name."

"I do know," I lied, and continued, "Do you think No Worries will still trade with you?"

"Sure he would," Kolorado said. "But, it's going to have to be a good trade. Do you have any trade goods?"

I explained about Morgan and Boyle.

"You have this all thought out," Kolorado said afterwards.

"We do."

"And what is that?" Kolorado beckoned at the pardon.

"This is a pardon from Judge Parker," I said. "You help us get that boy back, and it's yours. You'll never see the inside of a prison again."

Kolorado frowned and scratched his jaw.

"What about my livery stable? I can't just leave."

"Can't somebody else watch it for a few days?" I asked.

"Well, I reckon my wife could," Kolorado reasoned.

We were all startled.

"Your wife?" I asked.

"Sure. You didn't think I was married?"

"No," I said truthfully.

"Well, I am," Kolorado said. "Man with my looks couldn't stay a bachelor for long."

I didn't have an answer for that. Instead, I changed the subject.

"How long does it take to get to Bronc?" I asked.

"Depends how fast you travel."

"How 'bout two men with a mule?"

"Three days, give or take."

I frowned thoughtfully and looked at Cooper.

"They've got a day's start on us," I said.

"If they reach Bronc, it could ruin everything," Cooper replied.

"So we've got to overtake them," I figured.

"How?"

"Only way is if you and I take out in the morning without Jug-head," I said.

"What about Josie?" Cooper wanted to know.

I looked at Kolorado.

"Are you much of a tracker?"

"Depends how fresh the tracks are."

"If we left easy sign, could you follow me and Coop?"

"I could do that."

I nodded and looked at Cooper.

"We'll ride out in the morning, and Kolorado and Josie can bring Jug-head and follow at a slower pace."

Cooper frowned thoughtfully while I looked at Kolorado.

"Will that work?" I asked him.

"My wife won't like it, me being gone."

"You'll have to deal with your wife."

"Do I have any other choices?"

"No."

Kolorado scowled, but didn't reply.

"And if you try to run-," I warned.

"I won't run."

"So, we have a deal?"

"We have a deal," Kolorado nodded grudgingly.

"Good," I smiled.

Chapter twenty-one

After our talk, Kolorado hurried home while Cooper, Josie, and I walked down to the livery stable. It was late, so we rolled out our bedrolls.

We pulled our boots off and crawled in, and it fell silent. After a while I could hear the steady breathing of Josie as she slept.

"You asleep?" I heard Cooper's voice.

"Yes," I wisecracked.

"Kolorado sure didn't object much," Cooper said as he ignored my comment.

"No, he didn't."

"Makes you wonder why he had to change his name, doesn't it?"

"It does," I agreed.

"You trust him?"

I thought for a moment.

"I'm not sure," I finally said. "Do you?"

"I don't like the thought of leaving Josie with him."

"I can see how you'd feel that way," I said. "But, we don't have much choice."

"I reckon we don't," Cooper agreed. "I still don't like it though."

"Josie can take care of herself," I said. "She's a tough one."

"She is at that."

"Is she still mad?"

"Not so much. She's almost over it."

"I'm glad," I said. It was silent, and I asked carefully, "Does she still want to cook for us?"

"No. She said we were on our own."

I was glad it was dark, so that Cooper couldn't see the relieved look on my face.

"I could cook," I suggested.

"I figured you would. You usually do."
"It's settled then?"
"Sure."
I smiled, rolled over, and went to sleep.

Chapter twenty-two

It was still dark when we woke up. We rolled up our bedrolls, and I made a fire out back and cooked breakfast. Kolorado showed up, and I offered him a plate.

We ate, and afterwards we packed up everything and saddled our horses.

While Cooper said goodbye to Josie, I climbed on my horse and looked at Kolorado.

"We'll see you in a day or two," I said.

"We'll be along," Kolorado said.

I nodded, and then I waited for Cooper.

Josie looked worried as Cooper climbed on his horse.

"Be careful," she said.

"I'll take care of him," I said.

Josie smiled faintly, and we kicked up our horses.

***

We trotted out of town a ways, and then Cooper rode in a big circle, looking for tracks. There was nothing I could do to help, so I pulled up, laid my reins across my horse's neck, stuck my hands deep in my vest's pocket, hunched my shoulders, and watched.

It took a while, but Cooper finally found the tracks. He beckoned at me, and I grabbed my reins and kicked up my horse.

"Two horses and one mule," Cooper gestured at the ground as I rode up. "Going southwest."

"Should be them."

"Should be," Cooper agreed.

I nodded, and we fell into our routine.

The morning passed. We traveled in a brisk trot, and we made good time.

The country became rougher as we rode west. It was rocky and hilly, and there wasn't as much grass.

We rode across a stream around midday. We watered our horses and refilled our canteens with fresh water, and then we pushed on.

"Are we gaining on them?" I asked.

"Some," Cooper nodded.

"Reckon we'll catch them in time?"

"Not sure yet."

I nodded, and it fell silent.

Hour after hour passed. Cooper's eyes never left the ground, and mine never left the surrounding area.

We rode until it got so dark that Cooper couldn't see the tracks. We pulled up and made camp in a little gully.

"How close are we?" I asked while we unsaddled our horses.

"Getting pretty close," Cooper said. "I think we'll catch them tomorrow."

I frowned as I thought on that.

"Don't reckon we should have a fire then," I said, and Cooper nodded in agreement.

Soon as the horses were tended to, I unwrapped some leftover salt pork and biscuits. I divided it up between the two of us, and we sat on the ground as we ate.

"I've been thinking about Morgan and Boyle," I said after a while.

"What about 'em?"

"If it makes you feel better, we'll give them a chance to surrender."

Cooper looked at me and frowned.

"I thought that wasn't an option."

"It's not," I replied, and added, "They won't surrender anyway."

"How do you know?"

"I just know," I shrugged.

Cooper nodded thoughtfully, and it fell silent.

"I wonder how Kolorado and Josie are getting along," Cooper said after a while.

"I'm sure they're fine," I said.

"Do you reckon they're talking much?"

I smiled.

"That would be an interesting conversation," I said.

Chapter twenty-three

We were up before dawn. We ate a few cold biscuits, saddled our horses, and pushed on.

I watched the surrounding landscape with care. However, there were also a lot of things on my mind, and I couldn't help but frown as we rode along.

"What's the matter?" Cooper shot me a curious look.

"You really want to know?"

"I wouldn't have asked if I didn't."

I nodded, and then I sighed.

"Fourteen votes," I said. "Judge Parker told me that's all I got."

"That's all?"

"That's all."

Cooper whistled.

"When you lose, you sure lose big."

"After all we did for the folks at Midway, I figured I'd get more votes than that."

"Most folks have a short memory," Cooper replied. "Wagons saved the town from burning recently, and he also killed Stew. That made Wagons an instant hero, even if he really isn't."

"You think Wagons really killed Stew?"

"I believe he's dead."

"I still say Lee Mattingly had something to do with it."

"Do we have to go over that again?" Cooper frowned at me.

"No," I muttered.

"So, what else are you thinking about?"

I sighed again.

"Jessica," I admitted.

"What about her?"

"I can't get over how she *needs* to see Lee."

Cooper was silent for a bit, and then he cleared his throat.

"Lee was fond of Josie for a while too, remember?"

"He was," I agreed, and added, "But, the best man won."

"The best man will win this time too," Cooper declared.

"You think so?"

"I know so," Cooper said, and added, "Course, you've got to work on your conversation skills. Women like to talk."

"Josie doesn't."

"Josie ain't like most women," Cooper said.

I frowned thoughtfully, but didn't say anything.

Chapter twenty-four

Come midday we rode across a creek, and we stopped and watered our horses.

By midafternoon the tracks started getting fresh, and they turned to the south a bit. There was a steep mesa in front of us, and we had to ride slow as we climbed it.

It was late afternoon by the time we reached the top. We could see a long ways, so we stopped and studied the country.

Below us was a valley, and beyond that we could see the mountains in the far distance. There was a creek coming from the foothills, and the creek followed the valley.

"Nice layout," Cooper commented.

"Sure is."

"Remarkable how fast the country changes."

"It is."

"Those mountains should be in New Mexico."

"They are," I nodded.

"How far do you reckon those mountains are?"

"At least a day's ride; mebbe even two," I said.

"Valverde's Pass should be to the north."

"Yes, and Bronc is to the south," I said.

Cooper nodded, and it was silent as we studied the country some more.

"There's also a pass on the south side of the mountains," I said thoughtfully. "That's the pass Stew used, remember?"

Cooper nodded.

"When we leave Bronc, it would probably be shorter to go that way."

"Probably would," Cooper agreed.

"We'll keep that in mind," I said, and Cooper nodded.

We sat there a bit longer, and I suddenly spotted some movement. I leaned forward in the saddle and squinted.

"What is it?" Cooper asked.

"There," I pointed. "By the creek. There's something down there."

Cooper turned in the saddle, pulled out his spyglass, and squinted through it.

"I see them," Cooper finally announced. "Two men on horses, and a pack mule."

"There we are," I said softly.

"'We'?" Cooper asked, confused.

"That's going to be you and me down there," I explained.

Cooper frowned thoughtfully and nodded.

"I reckon it will be," he said.

"I'll be Morgan, and you'll be Boyle."

"How come you get to be Morgan?" Cooper shot me a dark look.

"I just assumed-," I started to say.

"What if Morgan is tall, dark, and handsome?" Cooper interrupted.

"What if he is?"

"If he is, then I should be Morgan, and you should be Boyle," Cooper declared, and added, "'Course, if he's small and boney, then you can be Morgan. We should stay close to the facts."

I frowned at Cooper.

"*If* he talks a lot," I said, "then you can be Morgan."

Cooper smiled, and asked, "What's the plan?"

"They'll probably camp by the creek."

"I'd say so."

"We'll wait 'til dark and ride up closer. Then we'll walk up to their camp on foot."

"Then what?"

"Then we'll do what we came here to do," I said.

Cooper frowned and nodded.

Chapter twenty-five

We stayed put until dark. We could see for miles, and we kept an eye on Morgan and Boyle with the eyeglass.

They stopped and camped beside the creek. They picketed their horses and built a fire, and as it got dark we could see the glow.

"Well, let's go," I said.

Cooper nodded. We climbed on our horses and followed an old cow trail.

Cooper and I were both solemn. There was no avoiding the confrontation that awaited, and that was a sobering thought.

We kept an eye on the glow of the campfire as we rode down the mesa. We came up beside the creek, and we followed it into the valley.

We stopped when we were a few hundred yards away. I could smell something cooking on the fire, and I also thought I could smell some coffee.

We dismounted and tied our horses to some nearby trees. Next, we checked our weapons. We both had our Colts, and Cooper carried his Henry.

"You ready?" I asked softly.

Cooper nodded.

I nodded back, and we walked towards the campfire. My gun hand hovered naturally over my gun-handle, and Cooper held his rifle with the barrel pointed down. I heard a soft click as he pulled the hammer back.

It was then that the feeling came all over me. I felt alert, calm, and ready. I glanced sideways at Cooper, and I could tell that he felt it too.

They heard us coming. They stood and spread out, and their hands hovered over their gun-handles.

"Hello the camp!" I called out.

"Who's out there?" One of them called back.

"There's two of us," I replied. "We're coming in."

It was silent, and then one of them replied, "Go ahead."

I glanced at Cooper. He nodded soberly, and we walked in and stopped at the outskirts of their camp. Cooper stood to my right.

It was silent while we studied each other.

One was bigger, and the other one was smaller. The smaller one stood in front of me, and he was very slim. Even in the dark I could tell that he had bright blue eyes, and he had an alert and graceful look about him.

The bigger one had a bit of a belly, with wide shoulders. He had a wide face, and his eyes were heavy-lidded. They looked so different that it was hard to believe they were brothers.

"Who might you be?" The smaller one asked, and he sounded very educated.

I reached into my pocket, pulled out my badge, pinned it on my vest's pocket, and gave it a little pat.

"Name's Yancy Landon," I announced. "This is my brother, Cooper. We're Texas Rangers."

"I've heard of you both," the smaller one said, and added, "I wasn't aware that you were Texas Rangers."

"It just happened," I said.

The smaller one nodded, and said, "I'm Morgan Gant, and this my brother, Boyle. You've probably heard of us."

"We have."

"I'd say we're on opposite sides of the law," Morgan smiled.

"You could say that."

"Interesting coincidence, us meeting like this."

"No coincidence. We trailed you from Landry," I corrected.

Morgan looked thoughtful. He glanced at Boyle and looked back at me.

"May I ask why?"

"You boys are trading rifles to the Injuns," I said.

Morgan looked surprised.

"Who told you that?"

"You've got two choices," I said as I ignored his question. "One; you both get on your horse and ride for California, and you never set foot in Texas again."

"And two?" Morgan asked, and there was sarcasm in his voice.

"You die."

Morgan chuckled.

"You overlooked choice number three."

"And what would that be?" I narrowed my eyes.

"We kill you."

"You could try."

"I've heard you're more than adequate with a Colt," Morgan said.

"You heard right."

"I'd like to see for myself, wouldn't you Boyle?"

Boyle nodded.

"There's no need for trouble," I said. "You boys can ride out for California."

"We aren't leaving," Morgan declared, and added, "So, that leaves us in a travesty."

I nodded.

"You boys were warned. I want you to remember that."

"We appreciate the warning," Morgan said, and it fell silent.

I watched Morgan. There was a twinkle in his eyes, but then they got hard. He blinked, and we both grabbed for our Colts.

With an easy movement, I palmed my Colt. The pistol boomed in my hand, and there was a loud thump as the bullet hit Morgan in the chest.

The impact propelled Morgan backwards. He had his Colt in his hand, and he managed to fire as he hit the ground. But, the bullet went harmlessly up into the air.

Gunshots erupted around me as I walked forward. Morgan tried to rise up and fire, but I fired before he could. My bullet caught him below the throat, and his body was flipped over backwards. He kicked out and was still.

I looked sideways. Cooper was standing there holding his Henry, and his eyes had a wild look to them. Boyle was lying on his back on the ground, and he was dead.

It was over.

There was a haze of gunpowder around us. I nodded at Cooper, and he nodded back and lowered his rifle.

I reloaded and holstered my Colt. Then, I walked over to Morgan's body.

Cooper joined me, and he frowned as we looked down at Morgan.

"You can be Morgan," he said in a somber voice.

Chapter twenty-six

It took a while for our nerves to settle. We walked back and got our horses, and we unsaddled and picketed them next to the other horses.

I dug my coffee cup out of my saddlebags and went over to the fire. The coffee pot was full, and I also noticed some salt pork in a frying pan. It was a little over-cooked, but not bad.

I poured myself some coffee, and Cooper walked up and frowned.

"You're drinking their coffee?"

"They won't be needing it," I gestured at them.

Cooper scratched his jaw thoughtfully.

"I reckon they won't," he agreed, and he went over to his saddlebags and dug out his cup.

"Grab our plates too," I told him.

Cooper returned to the fire, and I poured him a cup of coffee. Then, I split up the salt pork, and it was silent while we ate.

After supper, I poured myself another cup of coffee and leaned back. Meanwhile, Cooper pulled out his pipe and tobacco pouch. He packed it carefully, struck a match and lit it, and took a deep puff.

"Well, it's good to be alive," Cooper broke the silence.

"It is."

"Morgan sure did use a lot of fancy words."

"He did at that."

"What does adequate mean?"

"I'm not exactly sure," I replied.

"How 'bout travesty?"

"Not sure about that one neither," I admitted.

"Well, whatever it meant, they still had choices," Cooper said.

"They did."

"But, they chose the wrong choice."

"I'd say so."

"And it ain't our fault they chose the wrong choice."

"I even warned them," I added.

"You did," Cooper nodded.

"Does your conscience feel better now?" I asked.

"Not really. I still wish there'd been another way."

"Me too," I said softly.

Cooper took another puff on his pipe.

"So now what?"

"Come morning, we'll bury them," I said. "Then, we'll wait for Kolorado and Josie."

"They should be here tomorrow."

"Should be."

"What about Morgan and Boyle's horses?"

"We can't take them with us," I replied. "So, we'll pack all the supplies we can take and turn their horses loose. They should drift back to Landry."

"What about their saddles?"

"I reckon we'll have to leave them."

Cooper frowned as he thought on that.

"Seems like a waste," he said.

"It is a waste," I said. "But, there's nothing we can do about it."

"Reckon not," Cooper agreed.

I nodded and took another swig of coffee.

Chapter twenty-seven

I cooked breakfast at dawn. After we ate, we unpacked our shovels and buried Morgan and Boyle.

Cooper was silent while we worked. He kept glancing back to the east, and I could tell that he was worried.

After we got them buried, we went through their belongings. We packed all their supplies and food, and we piled everything that we couldn't take beside the graves. Their saddles and gear were among the pile.

It was midmorning by the time we finished everything. I rekindled the fire and made some more coffee. Soon as it was ready, I poured myself a cup and leaned back.

Cooper looked concerned as he squatted by the fire and poured himself a cup.

"Quit fretting. They'll show up," I said.

"They'd better," Cooper muttered, and added, "I'd still like to know why Kolorado was in prison."

"He was probably caught trading rifles to the Injuns," I suggested.

"Well, whatever he did, Josie's out there alone with him."

"Josie will be fine," I said.

"If they don't show up today, we're riding back east first thing in the morning," Cooper declared.

"Of course," I said.

Cooper nodded and took a swig of coffee.

"Been thinking," Cooper said after a while.

"Yes?"

"We're Texas Rangers," Cooper declared.

"That is correct."

"But, we're headed to New Mexico."

"That would also be correct," I nodded.

"Do we have jurisdiction in New Mexico?"

I frowned as I thought on that.

"I'm not really sure," I admitted.

"If we don't have jurisdiction, does that make what we're doing illegal?"

"No," I replied. "That makes it personal, but in a professional manner."

Cooper frowned, but didn't reply.

Chapter twenty-eight

It was midafternoon when Kolorado and Josie finally showed up.

We spotted them riding down the mesa, and a relieved look crossed Cooper's face.

It took them a while to reach us. Cooper waited anxiously, and he gave Josie a concerned look as they rode up.

"Are you all right?" He asked.

"We are fine," Josie said, and she frowned when she noticed the fresh graves. "What happened?"

"We caught 'em," Cooper explained with a solemn face.

A worried look crossed Josie's face.

"Are you hurt?"

"No, I'm fine," Cooper reassured.

Josie looked relieved.

"I'm good too," I added, but Josie didn't hear me. She was busy looking at Cooper.

I sighed and glanced at Kolorado. He had a pained expression on his face as he dismounted, and he limped over and sat by the campfire.

"What happened to you?" I asked curiously.

"I haven't rode this far in years," he explained.

I couldn't help but smile.

"Sore?"

Kolorado looked at me and scowled.

"I'll take care of your horse," I offered.

Kolorado grunted in response.

***

After the horses were tended to, I built the fire back up and cooked supper.

We didn't talk much while we ate. Afterwards, we drank some more coffee. It was late by then, so we turned in.

Kolorado grimaced as he stood, and he limped over to his bedroll and rolled it out. Next, he went over to his saddle and grabbed his rope. He circled his bedroll with the rope, and he pulled his boots off and crawled in.

I frowned as I watched him.

"What's the rope for?" I asked.

"Snakes."

"Snakes?"

"A snake will not cross a rope," Kolorado declared.

"Says who?" I challenged.

"Ask any old-timer; he'll tell you."

"I've heard of that," Cooper spoke up. "Didn't know if it was true or not."

"Course it's true," Kolorado grunted.

I shook my head as I thought on that.

"You are a very odd man," I said.

"I ain't never been snake bit neither," Kolorado replied, and he pulled his blankets up around him and rolled over.

I looked at Cooper. He and Josie were frowning at each other, and then Cooper walked over to his saddle and pulled his rope off.

"You aren't-," I frowned.

"I am."

"Surely you don't believe that."

"Doesn't matter," Cooper said. "What does matter is that I'm sleeping next to Kolorado, so anything that rope turns back will end up in my bed."

"This is ridiculous."

"I've heard of stranger things, Yancy."

"Just cause you hear things doesn't mean you have to believe them," I grunted, and I grabbed my bedroll and rolled it out.

"You ain't gonna?" Cooper looked at me curiously as I pulled my boots off and crawled into my bedroll.

"No, I ain't gonna."

"I hope you sleep well."

"I plan to," I replied, and I pulled my blankets up around me.

Chapter twenty-nine

I was the first one to wake up the next morning. I pulled my boots on and rolled up my bedroll, and then I stirred the coals and built the fire back up.

Everyone else awakened while I cooked breakfast, and I couldn't help but shake my head as I watched them coil their ropes up.

Everybody came up to the fire, and it was silent while we ate.

"Well, what's the plan?" Kolorado finally asked.

"Today's the day we're supposed to meet Ike's man," I said, and I glanced at Kolorado. "How far is Bronc?"

Kolorado thought for a moment.

"We should be there by midday," he said.

"Good," I said. "We'll ride to Bronc, and then me and Coop will ride on in."

"What if Ike's man ain't there?" Kolorado wanted to know.

"Then we'll wait 'til he shows up."

"Can I go home if he doesn't show up?"

"No."

Kolorado scowled, but didn't say anything else.

We finished breakfast, and then we packed up camp and saddled our horses. We also turned Morgan and Boyle's horses loose, but we kept the mule.

"Well, look at that!" Cooper suddenly exclaimed.

We all turned and looked, and Cooper was pointing at the ground where my bedroll had been.

We walked over, and in the sand were fresh snake tracks.

"What'd I tell you?" Kolorado exclaimed.

I looked at Cooper. His eyes were twinkling, and I frowned suspiciously.

"You made those tracks," I accused.

Cooper didn't reply. Instead, he just chuckled as he walked over to his horse and mounted up.

I stood there a moment, and then I scowled as I walked over to my horse.

Chapter thirty

We arrived at Bronc around midday, just as Kolorado had said.

There were a lot of rolling hills surrounding Bronc. The tallest hill had a lot of brush, so we rode to the top and dismounted. Cooper pulled out his spyglass, and we studied the town.

Bronc made Landry look like a boomtown. There were only three buildings. There was a livery stable, a trading post, and a cantina.

"Ain't much of a town," Cooper commented.

"Ike's man shouldn't be hard to find then," I said.

"*If* he's there."

"True."

"Where do you suppose he is?"

"Probably the cantina."

"Reckon we should go find out."

"I reckon we should," I agreed, and I looked at Kolorado and Josie. "You two stay here. I'm not sure when we'll be back, but try your best not to be seen. Don't build a campfire."

"What if it gets dark?" Kolorado asked.

"Then it gets dark."

Kolorado scowled while Cooper and I climbed on our horses.

"We'll be back," I said.

Josie looked at Cooper, and he smiled reassuringly. She smiled back, and then they watched us as we rode down the hill.

***

I'm not sure why, but I felt uncomfortable as we rode in, and I could tell that Cooper felt it too.

The street was dry and dusty, and flies buzzed around us. There was also a stink that rose up from the ground.

Cooper frowned as he looked around.

"I don't see any other horses tied to hitching posts," he commented.

"Or two mules, packed with rifles," I added.

He nodded, and we rode up to the cantina and pulled up.

There were three men sitting on the porch. One was tall, one was short, and the other was fat. All three wore shabby clothes, and they also smelled. They were chewing tobacco, and they spat on the sidewalk as they stared at us.

We stared back, and several seconds passed.

"Afternoon," I finally said.

The fat one nodded, but that was all.

I glanced at Cooper, and then we dismounted. We tied our horses to the rail, stepped up on the porch, and walked through the swinging doors. The three men just sat there and watched us.

We paused at the doorway while our eyes adjusted, and then we looked around.

The cantina wasn't much of a place. It was dark, and it smelled of whiskey, sweat, and cigar smoke. There were a few tables spread about, and the bar was two long planks laid on top of two whiskey kegs.

The place was empty except for us and a fat Mexican that stood behind the bar. He looked unconcerned and uninterested as we stopped in front of him.

"Have any other strangers been in here?" I asked.

He looked at me with a blank look.

"Speak-idy any English?" I raised my voice.

"Whiskey?" He asked with a thick accent.

"Coffee'll do."

"No whiskey?"

"Coffee," I said louder. "You *savvy* coffee?"

"I make," he said.

I nodded, and Cooper and I walked to the back and sat down at a table. Cooper leaned his rifle in the corner, and we positioned ourselves so that we could see the entire room.

"I wonder why we do that," Cooper commented.

"Do what?"

"Speak louder when someone doesn't understand what we're saying, as if that'll help."

I frowned at Cooper, and he smiled.

A few minutes passed, and the Mexican brought us a pot of coffee and two cups.

"Do you have any sugar?" I asked.

He gave me a blank look.

"Never mind," I said, and he nodded and returned to the bar.

Cooper smiled at me as he poured us both a cup. We took a cautious swig, and Cooper nodded.

"It ain't too bad," he said.

"It ain't too good neither," I grumbled.

"Better than nothing."

"It is," I agreed.

Cooper nodded and changed the subject.

"I didn't like the looks of them fellers outside."

"Can't say I did neither."

"You reckon they're Ike's men?"

"We'll know soon enough."

Cooper nodded again, and it fell silent.

Time passed slowly. We each drank three cups, and then we heard a noise from outside.

It was a horse, trotting into town. But then the horse stopped, and Cooper and I glanced at each other.

Seconds later, the swinging doors burst open, and we could see the silhouette of a man standing in the doorway. A few seconds passed, and he stepped inside.

He took a slow look around the room. His gaze finally came to us, and he narrowed his eyes. His face was emotionless, and his eyes were hard.

He walked over to the bar, and I frowned as I studied him. He was dark, lean, and hard looking. I wasn't sure, but he looked half Mexican and half Indian.

He spoke softly to the Mexican behind the bar. It was in Spanish. The Mexican gave him a bottle and a glass, and he paid for it and filled his glass.

He took a swig, and then he turned around and stared at us. There was nothing else to look at, so we stared back.

Several minutes passed. He took several swigs of whiskey, but he never took his eyes off us. There was a scornful look in his eyes, and I could tell that he was studying us, as if he was wondering who he should shoot first.

I held my coffee cup in my left hand. I took a swig, and as I did I lowered my right hand over my gun handle, just in case.

He noticed my movements, and I heard a slight grunt of amusement.

I set my coffee cup down and smiled at him. He ignored my smile as he took another swig of whiskey.

"Why's he staring at us?" Cooper whispered, and I could barely hear his voice.

"You want to ask him?" I whispered back.

Cooper frowned, but didn't reply.

More time passed. We drank more coffee, and the half-breed drank more whiskey. He never took his eyes off us. His face was very solemn, and I could tell that he didn't like us.

Suddenly, he took a big gulp of whiskey and finished his drink. He slammed the cup down on the bar, looked at us and grinned, and walked briskly towards the door. He shoved the swinging doors open and walked out, and we heard him as he mounted up and rode out.

Cooper looked at me with a startled look.

"Who was that?"

"Not sure. He looked like a half-breed."

"Do you think that was our man?"

"I hope not."

"I wonder why he left?"

"Mebbe we scared him," I suggested.

"So now what?"

"We wait," I said.

Chapter thirty-one

Another hour passed. We drank another pot of coffee, and then we just sat there.

I studied the Mexican behind the bar. He stood perfectly still, and I couldn't help but wonder how he could stay in one position for so long.

We finally heard the sound of several horses coming into town. A few seconds passed, and we heard someone step up onto the porch of the cantina.

I glanced at Cooper, and then we watched the swinging doors. They opened, and in stepped a tall man. He paused at the door, and then he walked over to the bar.

He was a very big man. I figured he stood over six feet tall, and he had a muscled torso with dark hair.

There was a cocky way about him, and I could tell that he had a high opinion of himself.

He ignored us as he bought a bottle of whiskey. He grabbed a glass, poured himself a drink, took a deep swig, and then turned and looked at us.

He finished his drink, poured himself another, and walked over.

"Morgan and Boyle Gant?" He asked.

"That's us," I said.

"I wasn't sure where to look for you."

"Ain't that many choices in this town," I said.

He nodded and puffed out his chest.

"I'm Brock Jackson."

"You Ike's man?"

Brock frowned as he sat down.

"I thought you boys already understood everything."

I glanced at Cooper and frowned.

"Understand what?"

Brock glanced at the Mexican behind the bar and lowered his voice.

"Ike doesn't want his name to be mentioned. Not here, not anywhere. You understand?"

"Of course," I said. "We forgot."

"Well don't forget again," Brock warned.

I forced a smile and nodded.

"All right," Brock said. "I've got two mules outside, packed with rifles. We'll meet back here in eight weeks. You bring back *all* the pelts, and I'll pay you your share and give you more rifles."

"Sounds good," I nodded.

Brock nodded, and he took another swig of whiskey and frowned at us.

"You boys ain't exactly what I was expecting," he said.

"How's that?" I frowned.

"I've heard plenty of talk about Morgan Gant," he said. "He's elegant, and he speaks big, fancy words that no one understands. But, I understand you very well."

"I've been working on that."

"Are you any good with that?" He gestured at my Colt.

I thought a moment before I replied.

"I'm adequate," I said.

Brock grunted wolfishly, and he finished his drink in one gulp.

"Well, I reckon we're done here," he said.

"We'll be on our way then," I said.

"I almost forgot. Rocca should be along soon."

"Rocca?" I frowned.

"Nobody told you about Rocca?" Brock frowned at us.

"Remind us."

"He's half Mexican and half Injun," Brock informed. "We hired him to take you to the Injun's camp. He speaks Apache."

"Where is he?" I asked.

"I don't know. He's supposed to be here."

"I think he was here a while ago," I said thoughtfully. "He came in, had a few drinks, and left."

92

"That's how Rocca is," Brock said. "Don't worry; he'll find you."

"We don't need him," I said abruptly.

"Why not?" Brock looked startled.

"We have our own man," I explained, and I looked at Cooper. "Ain't that right, Boyle?"

Cooper's face remained blank.

"*Boyle*," I said sharply.

Cooper looked startled, and he jumped in his chair.

"Oh. Yes. That is correct," he said.

I frowned at him and looked back at Brock.

"So Rocca isn't needed," I said.

Brock snorted as he stood.

"I don't care if you use him or not," he said. "All that matters is that you're back here in eight weeks with those pelts."

"So you'll get rid of Rocca?"

"No. I'll let you do that," Brock grinned, and he turned and walked towards the door.

Cooper and I looked at each other and frowned, and then we followed Brock outside.

The tall man, the short man, and the fat man were still sitting on the porch. They were also still chewing tobacco, and they were studying the mules.

Brock had tied his horse and the two mules beside ours. Each mule was packed with two crates.

We got mounted. Cooper led one mule, and I led the other one. I glanced over at the porch, and all three men were still staring at the mules with solemn faces.

I glanced at Brock.

"We'll be seeing you," I said.

"Sure," Brock said, and he kicked up his horse and headed south.

I watched him go, and then I looked once more at the men on the porch. I nodded at them, and the fat one nodded back.

We kicked up our horses and left town in a walk. I could feel the eyes of the men on the porch watching us, and I knew that trouble was coming.

Chapter thirty-two

"What'd you think of those men on the porch?" Cooper asked me as we rode to the top of the hill.

"I thought they needed a bath," I replied.

"They sure seemed curious."

"Too curious," I agreed.

"Think they'll be trouble?"

"I think we'd better plan for it," I said.

"I was afraid of that."

I nodded, and it fell silent as we rode on.

It was about a three-mile ride up to the top of the hill. Josie looked relieved when she saw us, but Kolorado scowled.

"Took you long enough," he said.

"It did," I agreed, and I looked over at Cooper. "Can I borrow your spyglass?"

"Sure," Cooper said, and he dug it out of his saddlebags and handed it to me.

We dismounted, and I walked to the edge of the hill and squatted behind some bushes. From there I kept an eye on Bronc.

"What are you looking for?" Kolorado asked me.

"Trouble," I replied.

Kolorado waited for me to explain, and he muttered to himself when I didn't.

A few minutes passed. Kolorado started getting impatient, but I ignored him.

Finally, I saw what I was looking for. Three men on horses rode out of town going north, and I frowned as I studied them through the spyglass.

"It's them," I told Cooper.

"They'll probably ride out a few miles, and then start hunting for our tracks," Cooper figured.

"I'd say so," I nodded.

"Why would they come after us?" Kolorado wanted to know.

"They're probably curious to know what's in those crates," I gestured at the mules.

"What are we gonna do?" Kolorado asked.

I thought on that for a moment.

"We're going to let them find us," I finally said.

***

We mounted up and rode north. The mules slowed us some, and a brisk walk was all we could manage.

A couple of hours passed, and the sun started to disappear behind the mountains. We were now in rolling hills, and there was a lot of brush and cover.

We rode into a dry gully, and I looked around and nodded.

"This is a likely place," I said. "We'll camp here."

We dismounted, and I gestured at a clear spot.

"We'll build a big fire there, out in the open."

Cooper looked at me and frowned.

"What exactly do you have in mind, Yancy?"

"Well, I figure we'll roll our bedrolls out by the fire, puff them up a little, and then hide out in the bushes and wait."

"Seems like a mighty simple plan to me," Kolorado objected.

"We're dealing with simple minded folks," I replied. "We get all tricky, and it'll throw them off. It'll make 'em use common sense, and that's the last thing we want."

Kolorado frowned uncertainly, but didn't reply.

"Anybody hungry?" I asked. "We've got time to cook supper."

"I ain't hungry," Kolorado replied, and Cooper and Josie shook their heads.

"Well, think I'll make some coffee anyhow," I said.

Everybody got busy. Josie and Kolorado took care of the horses and mules, and Cooper rolled out the bedrolls. Meanwhile, I built a fire and put the coffee on.

The coffee was ready by the time everybody finished. I poured a cup for everyone, and then I put a few more branches on the fire and built it up bigger.

We walked out into the bushes and found some cover. Coop, Josie, and I sat behind a log while Kolorado sat between two shrubs and leaned against a tree.

Cooper's rifle was laid out in front of him, and I had ahold of my Colt. Josie had her bow and arrows, and Kolorado held his rifle.

The night air was cool, and Cooper and Josie huddled together. I was cold, but I didn't show it.

A couple of hours passed, and it got colder. Finally, Cooper glanced at me.

"Where are they?" he whispered.

"Mebbe they're waiting to make sure we're asleep," I suggested.

"I thought you said these were simple minded folks."

"Well, they sure looked simple minded," I replied.

"I can't argue that."

"Are we gonna stay out here all night?" Kolorado spoke up.

"If we have to," I replied.

"I don't think they're coming."

"We'll know soon enough," I said, and added, "Now be quiet."

Kolorado grunted, and it fell silent.

Chapter thirty-three

Another hour came and went.

By now I was stiff. My back ached, and my legs felt cramped. But, I didn't dare move.

I heard a soft snore. I glanced at Cooper and Josie, and they heard it too.

Kolorado was out. His head was leaned back against the tree, and his rifle rested in his lap.

Cooper looked at me, but I shook my head.

"Let him sleep," I said softly. "We've got ahold of things."

Cooper nodded, and he rubbed his shoulders and shivered.

"Remarkable, how cool it gets up here at night," he whispered.

"It is," I agreed.

"Fire sure does look warm."

"It does."

"Be sorta funny if they don't show up."

"How's that?"

"You know. Us sitting here, all cold like, and looking at a warm fire all night."

"I don't see the humor in that."

"I just wish they'd hurry up," Cooper murmured wistfully.

"Mebbe they froze to death."

I heard Cooper grunt softly.

"We could be wrong about this," he said.

"I don't think so. They looked greedy to me."

"But they could have gone way ahead of us, and be waiting to ambush us tomorrow," Cooper suggested.

"That's a strong possibility."

"I reckon we'll find out soon enough."

"Reckon we will," I agreed.

Cooper nodded, and it fell silent.

Another thirty minutes passed. The fire started to go out, but I didn't want to chance moving to build it back up.

Suddenly, I heard something in front of us. But I wasn't sure what I'd heard, and I cocked my head sideways as I listened.

I heard something again, only this time it was behind us. I heard it again, and I knew that somebody was walking towards us.

"Coop," I whispered tersely. "Behind us!"

Cooper nodded. He pulled the hammer back on his rifle, and it made a soft click. Meanwhile, Josie placed an arrow in her bow and held it ready.

We listened as they got closer.

From experience, I knew that Cooper was waiting on me to make a move. But I waited, because I wanted to draw them in closer.

A rifle shot suddenly boomed out, and I heard a thumping sound as it hit flesh.

With a surprised yell, I jumped to my feet and spun around with my Colt in my hand.

The tall man stood in front of us, and he was holding his rifle. He was just as startled as we were, and I shot him before he could recover. Cooper shot him too, and his body was flung backwards.

I spotted the short man to my left. He had his rifle up, but an arrow struck him in the chest before he could get a shot off. I heard a gasp of pain, and he dropped his rifle and staggered backwards. He grabbed for his Colt, but I shot him as he brought it up. There was a loud thump as the bullet connected, and he was flipped over backwards.

It was silent, and then we heard another rifle shot. It was close, and we all jumped.

It was Kolorado. He was sitting on the ground, and he was holding his rifle with the barrel pointed up. He looked confused and scared.

"Watch where you're pointing that thing!" I glared at him.

Kolorado looked at me but didn't reply. Meanwhile, I glanced at Cooper.

"I heard something over there," I gestured.

Cooper nodded, and he and Josie crouched down and went that way while I turned towards the two men that we had shot.

I walked out a ways, and I spotted another body. It was the fat man, and he lay on his back. He had been shot in the chest, and he was dead.

Kolorado joined me. He was out of breath and was panting hard.

"What just happened?" He asked.

"I'm not sure," I replied.

Cooper and Josie walked up a couple of minutes later, and I gave Cooper a questioning look.

"There was nobody there," Cooper shook his head.

"I know I heard something," I insisted.

"Well, whoever it was, they're gone now."

I nodded, and then I pointed at the fat one.

"Who shot this one?"

Josie shook her head, and Cooper looked at him and frowned.

"I never even saw him," he admitted.

"Me neither," I replied.

"I think I did," Kolorado spoke up. It was silent, and he added, "Yes, I'm sure of it now."

"You're sure?" I frowned at him.

"Course I'm sure!" he fired back.

I glanced at Cooper, but he just shrugged.

"So now what?" Kolorado asked.

"Excitement's over for now," I said. "I reckon we can turn in."

"I don't think I could make myself sleep now," Kolorado objected.

I smiled and nodded.

"Well, we've got three graves to dig," I suggested.

"Might as well get it over with," Cooper spoke up, and everyone nodded in agreement.

"I'll unpack the shovels," I said.

Chapter thirty-four

There's nothing like hard work to make you tired.

It took us a couple of hours to get them all buried. Afterwards, Cooper and I walked out and looked for their horses, but we couldn't find them.

"They probably broke loose when the shooting started," Cooper figured.

"If they did, they'll be back at Bronc by morning," I said.

"I'm just glad our horses didn't run off," Cooper said.

"We probably tied ours better."

Cooper nodded, and we trudged back to camp. Kolorado was sitting by the fire, and he looked exhausted.

"It'll be daylight in a few hours," I told everybody. "We might as well get some sleep."

"Should one of us keep watch?" Cooper asked.

"We'll be all right tonight," I replied.

Everybody nodded, and we climbed into our bedrolls. A few minutes passed, and we all slipped off to sleep.

***

I woke to the sound of chirping. The sun was up, and I rubbed my eyes as I sat up.

A flock of birds was nestling around us. They were small, with black bodies and bright, yellow breasts.

I glanced at Cooper. He was sitting up in his bedroll, and he was frowning at them.

"Loud little fellers, ain't they," he said.

"They are," I nodded.

"Them's rain birds," Kolorado declared from his bedroll.

"Rain birds?"

"Yep. When you see them, just know that a big rain is coming. Usually within three days."

"How do you come up with all of this?" I frowned at him.

"Everybody knows that," Kolorado replied.

I thought on that for a moment.

"So where do these rain birds go when it's not raining?" I challenged.

"I reckon they go wherever it *is* raining," Kolorado replied stubbornly.

I grunted, and I pulled my boots on and rolled up my bedroll.

My movements caused the birds to fly away. However, there was a slender, brown looking bird that stayed.

"Is that a rain bird too?" I gestured, and my voice was thick with sarcasm.

"No, that's a mile-or-more bird," Kolorado squinted at him.

"Mile-or-more bird?"

"Sure," he nodded. "They pass a lot of gas, and you can hear it from a mile-or-more."

I sighed, but didn't reply.

Chapter thirty-five

While I cooked breakfast, Cooper walked out a ways and looked for tracks. He showed back up as I was making everyone a plate.

"You were right," he told me. "There was somebody else out there last night."

"I thought so."

"I found his tracks behind some bushes over there. I backtracked him to where he'd tied his horse."

"I wonder who he was?" Kolorado spoke up.

"Rocca," I figured.

"Who?"

"He's a feller that trades with the Injuns. He's supposed to be our guide."

"I thought that was my job," Kolorado said.

"It is."

Kolorado looked confused, but he didn't say anything more.

"I also found this behind the bushes," Cooper said, and he held up an empty bullet shell.

"So he's the one who fired the first shot," I surmised.

"I'd say so," Cooper nodded.

I glanced at Kolorado, and he scowled.

"Well," I said thoughtfully. "That's good to know."

Cooper nodded, and it fell silent as we ate.

***

We saddled up after breakfast and rode out. Cooper led the way, and Josie followed him. Kolorado was next, and I brought up the rear. Each one of us led a mule.

The morning passed smoothly. We rode towards the pass on the south side of the mountains, and we reached the foothills by midday. There was a stream there, and we stopped and watered our stock.

Cooper looked wistful as we looked up at the mountains.

"What is it?" I asked.

"Every time I go up there," Cooper explained, "I get shot."

"You getting superstitious?"

"No. It's bad luck to be superstitious."

I smiled.

"Just stick close to me," I said. "And you'll be fine."

"I hope so," Cooper replied, and we kicked up our horses and entered the pass.

Chapter thirty-six

It was a steep climb into the mountains. There was a trail that led upwards, and Cooper let his horse follow it.

The landscape changed quickly. It became very rocky, and trees were all about. It was also a lot cooler.

The afternoon passed. We made good time, and by evening time we were high in the mountains.

"There should be a big lakebed up ahead," I told Cooper. "That's where Lee killed Stew's men. Remember?"

"I wasn't there," Cooper reminded.

"I know, but I told you about it," I frowned, and continued, "That would be a good place to camp."

Cooper nodded, and we rode on.

We reached the lakebed right as it was getting dark. The lakebed was in a meadow, and there was a line of trees that surrounded it.

We rode through the trees and entered the lakebed. While everyone else made camp, I built a fire and cooked supper.

After supper, I stood and walked over to the crates of rifles.

"I reckon we should disable these," I suggested. "We might not have the time later."

Kolorado didn't like that idea, but he still got to his feet and walked over.

"How do you disable them?" He asked.

I opened a crate, picked up a rifle, and showed him.

"It's simple," I instructed. "You unscrew the side plate, and then you unscrew this tiny screw here. That loosens the carrier spring, and you can pull the spring right out."

"That's it?"

"That's it," I nodded.

We developed a routine. Kolorado unpacked the rifles, and Cooper and I disabled them. Josie re-packed the rifles, and she made sure that she left untouched rifles at the top of each crate.

It took us a couple of hours to finish. We were thirsty afterwards, so I built the fire back up and made some coffee.

We sat around the fire and drank a few cups. Afterwards, Cooper needed to go out into the bushes, and he disappeared amongst the trees.

"Yancy," he said after a moment.

I walked towards his voice.

"Yes?"

"What do you make of that?"

I walked up beside Cooper, and he pointed to the south. There, in the far distance, was a faint glow.

"Looks like a campfire," I said thoughtfully.

"How far do you reckon it is?" Cooper said.

"Mebbe a mile," I figured.

"We rode through there today," Cooper said, and asked, "You reckon they're following us?"

I scratched my jaw as I thought on that.

"Probably are," I said.

"I wonder who it is?"

"Only one person I can think of," I replied.

"Rocca?"

I nodded.

"What do we do?" Cooper asked.

"Let's go find out," I said.

Chapter thirty-seven

We left Josie and Kolorado at the lakebed. They didn't like it, but I didn't want Kolorado to be in the way.

We saddled our horses and took out. It was so dark that we couldn't even see the ground, so we had to ride slow.

We pulled up when we were a few hundred yards away. We dismounted, tied our horses to some trees, and crept towards the campfire. Cooper held his rifle, and my Colt was in my holster.

We stopped and studied the campfire when we got closer.

We could only see one horse picketed out. A man sat by the fire, and he was drinking coffee.

"Recognize him?" I asked in a whisper.

"That's the feller from the cantina," Cooper whispered back, and added, "Rocca."

I nodded, and it was silent as I thought on the situation.

"I'll have a talk with him," I finally said. "Why don't you circle in behind and cover us with your Henry."

Cooper nodded. He crouched down and took off.

I watched him go, and then I checked my Colt. I returned it to my holster, and I waited for Cooper to get in position.

About five minutes passed, and then I walked towards the campfire.

"Hello the camp!" I called out.

Without a word, the man dropped his coffee cup, rolled over, grabbed his rifle, and came up on his feet.

"Hold your fire!" I said tersely. "We don't want trouble."

He stood still as he thought on that, and then he lowered the rifle. I nodded and walked on in.

He recognized me, and a scornful smirk crossed his face.

"It is you," he said in a thick, Spanish accent.

"That's right."

"I see you do not die today. That is good."

"I'll agree with that," I said, and added, "My brother's out there with a rifle. I reckon you understand what that means."

He smiled.

"I do not wish for trouble, *senor*. Not yet."

"Yet?"

"You are Morgan Gant."

"I am," I nodded.

"I am Rocca."

"I figured you was," I said.

"I am your guide."

"We need to discuss that."

"My father's name was Pancho Esperanza," he suddenly declared.

"Was?"

"He is dead now."

"I'm sorry to hear that."

"You do not know of my father?" He looked at me curiously.

I thought for a moment.

"No," I said.

"You are sure?"

"Yes," I replied.

Rocca snorted, and it was silent for a moment.

"You were at our camp last night," I changed the subject.

A surprised looked crossed his face.

"You saw me?"

"No, I heard you," I said. "You shot the fat one."

Rocca smiled.

"He was fat."

"I appreciate the help, but why did you leave?"

"I do not like you."

"How come?"

"My father."

"I notice you keep mentioning him. Why?"

"You do not remember?"

"Remember what?" I frowned.

"You killed him."

I was startled, and several seconds passed as I thought on that.

"No," I finally said. "I did not."

"You lie," he said, and his eyes flashed angrily. "They told me. It was you, Morgan Gant."

I didn't know how to answer that, so I was silent.

"That is why I take this job," Rocca declared. "To meet you."

"So you can kill me?"

"Maybe," Rocca said. "Or, maybe I steal your business. You cannot trade with the Apache. But Rocca can."

"You're wrong there. I can trade with the Apaches," I said, and added, "It is you that's not needed. I told Brock that, but he said for me to tell you."

The scornful look returned to Rocca's face.

"You wish me to go?"

"That is correct."

"No one tells Rocca to go."

"Well, I'm telling you now."

Rocca frowned, and it fell silent as we studied each other.

"I understand," Rocca finally said.

"That is good," I said. "We'll be leaving now, and don't try to follow us."

Rocca didn't reply, and his face remained blank.

"And I don't care what you heard," I said. "I didn't kill your father."

A stubborn look crossed Rocca's face.

"I have nothing else to say," he said.

"Neither do I," I said.

Rocca nodded. I backed up some, and then I turned and disappeared into the darkness.

Chapter thirty-eight

I walked back to the horses and waited for Cooper. Soon as he got there, we mounted up and rode north.

"Did you hear everything?" I asked him.

"I sure did."

"He thinks I killed his father."

"Why didn't you tell him you weren't Morgan?"

"I couldn't," I replied.

"Why not?"

"A feller like Rocca will do anything for money," I said. "If he found out who I really was, he'd run to Ike."

"I'm a little surprised you didn't shoot him."

"It did cross my mind," I admitted.

"What stopped you?"

"After what he did for us last night, I figured I ought to give him a chance," I explained.

"Give him a chance to do what? Kill you?"

"No. Give him a chance to leave."

"I reckon he did save us."

"I wouldn't go that far," I frowned. "He helped us. That's all."

"He probably wanted to save you for himself."

"It's possible."

"Do you think he'll leave now?"

"No," I said.

Cooper frowned thoughtfully, but he didn't say anything else.

It didn't take us long to get back to our camp. Kolorado was full of questions, and Cooper explained what happened.

"What happens next?" Kolorado wanted to know.

"We go to bed," I said.

"That's not what I meant," Kolorado frowned.

"Well, in the morning we'll head north," I said.

"What about this Rocca feller?" Kolorado asked.

"What about him?" I asked.

"Shouldn't we do something?"

"No," I replied, and added, "Go ahead and turn in. I'll keep watch for a while."

Kolorado grumbled something as he rolled out his bedroll and crawled in. Cooper and Josie did the same, and soon all three were asleep.

My watch went smoothly, and Cooper relieved me a few hours later. I rolled out my bedroll, pulled my boots off, and crawled in. I was tired, and I went right to sleep.

***

A buzzing sound woke me the next morning. I stirred, but then the sound went away. I yawned, rubbed my eyes, and turned over.

The buzzing sound came back, only it sounded more irritable this time.

I was suddenly wide-awake. I looked sideways and spotted a rattlesnake a few feet from me. He was coiled and ready to strike.

"Don't move," a calm, stern voice said.

Cooper stood behind the snake, and he held a long, thick branch. In one move, he swept the snake away from me. The snake struck at Cooper, but he delivered a deathblow to the back of his head with the branch. He hit him a few more times for good measure, and then he looked at me.

My hands shook as I crawled out of my bedroll.

"Thanks," I managed to say.

"That was a close one," Cooper said.

"Too close," I agreed.

"What'd I tell you?" Kolorado exclaimed from his bedroll.

I glared at Kolorado.

"Don't say a word," I warned.

Kolorado tried to look hurt while I looked at Cooper and Josie. I could tell that they were trying not to grin.

"This could have happened to any of us," I said irritably.

"But it didn't," Cooper replied. "It happened to you."

"It was just a coincidence," I retorted.

Nobody said anything. Instead, they just glanced at each other.

"Having a rope around my bed would have made no difference," I declared.

They were silent.

"It makes no sense," I tried again. "And, if you think I'm going to start putting a rope around my bed, you are mistaken."

Nobody replied. Instead, they all looked down at the ground.

"I'm disappointed in you, Coop. Every time Kolorado tells us some far-fetched yarn, you cleave to it for solemn fact."

Cooper nodded and smiled.

"Why isn't anybody saying anything?" I demanded to know.

"You told me not to," Kolorado spoke up.

I scowled at him, but didn't say anything.

Chapter thirty-nine

It took a while for the nerves to settle, but I finally got around to cooking breakfast. We ate, and afterwards we packed up camp. Next, we saddled our horses and packed the mules.

We climbed into the saddle, and Kolorado pointed at the snake.

"Look at that," he said.

"Look at what?" I frowned.

"That snake has turned belly up."

"So?"

"When you kill a snake and he turns belly up, it means it's going to rain," he declared.

I scowled, but didn't reply. Instead, I looked at Cooper and motioned for him to lead out. Cooper grinned and kicked up his horse, and everyone fell in behind him.

We rode in silence for a couple of hours, and then Cooper turned in the saddle and looked back at me.

"Do you remember the cabin that you and Rondo stayed at?"

I nodded.

"It should be up ahead," Cooper recollected.

"It is. We'll be there this afternoon," I said.

"It'd be nice to sleep indoors for a change," Cooper said, and added, "Especially if it rains."

"It would," I agreed, and I looked at Josie. "How far is the Apache's camp from the cabin?"

Josie pinched her face in thought.

"A day and a half," she said.

"Good," I said.

It fell silent as we traveled on. The mules became difficult, so we didn't make very good time.

We rode across a creek midafternoon. We stopped and watered our stock, and then we pushed on. We arrived at the cabin late afternoon.

It was a small cabin, nestled in amongst several trees. There was also a small corral made of logs and a lean-to where saddles could be kept. On the other side of the cabin were several unmarked graves.

"This is the place," I said thoughtfully as we pulled up.

"This is what place?" Kolorado looked at me.

I was silent, so Cooper explained.

"This is where Stew Baine was killed by Sheriff Wagons."

"The man who killed Stew Baine," Kolorado said softly.

"That's the story," I said. "But, I think something else happened."

"Like what?" Kolorado asked.

"I don't know," I grumbled, and added, "One of these days, I'm going to find out."

Cooper looked at me and frowned, but I ignored him as we dismounted.

We walked inside the cabin and looked around. It was dusty, and there were a few cobwebs. Other than that, the cabin was in good shape, and there was also a fireplace.

"I will clean up," Josie offered.

I nodded and turned towards the door.

"We'll take care of the horses," I said.

Josie nodded, and we all got busy.

We unpacked the mules and placed the rifles under the lean-to. Then, while Cooper and Kolorado tended to the horses, I gathered some wood and built a fire inside. I cooked supper and made some coffee, and we sat around the fireplace and ate.

"Snug little cabin," Cooper commented as he glanced around.

"It is," Josie said, and she looked at Cooper and smiled.

"It's too bad we couldn't pick this cabin up and put it wherever we wanted," Cooper said wistfully.

Josie smiled faintly, and it was silent as we finished supper.

Afterwards, we drank some more coffee, and then we rolled out our bedrolls.

"I'll take the first watch," Cooper offered.

"I watch with you?" Josie asked hopefully.

"Sure," Cooper said, and he looked at me. "I'll wake you up around midnight."

I nodded, and Cooper and Josie walked out the door.

I glanced at Kolorado. He had already pulled his boots off and was crawling into his bedroll.

"Night," he said.

"Sure," I said.

I watched him for a moment, and then I pulled my own boots off and crawled into my bedroll.

Chapter forty

Cooper woke me at midnight. I yawned as I pulled my boots on, and I joined Cooper and Josie outside.

"Look," Cooper gestured to the south.

There, in the far distance, was the faint glow of a campfire.

"Rocca," I said with a frown.

"We spotted it a few hours ago." Cooper said. "Looks like he's still following us."

"I'd say so," I agreed.

It was silent for a bit, and I cleared my throat.

"He wants us to see him," I said.

"Why do you say that?"

"That fire should have burned out hours ago. He's keeping it going so we'll see it."

"Why does he want to be seen?"

"Mebbe he's sending us a message," I figured. "He wants us to know that he ain't afraid of us."

"He might be hoping we'll come visit again," Cooper suggested.

"Could be."

"What do we do?"

"Nothing," I replied. "You and Josie get some sleep. I'll keep watch."

"I could sure sleep."

"Go ahead then."

Cooper nodded, and he and Josie walked towards the cabin.

I watched them go, and then I settled down next to the lean-to.

***

The campfire finally faded out a couple of hours later, so I figured Rocca finally went to sleep. I was sleepy myself, but I forced myself to stay awake.

The night passed smoothly. I finally heard a noise over by the cabin, but it was only Kolorado. He held his rifle, and he walked over and offered to keep watch.

"It'll be daylight in a couple of hours," I objected.

"Go ahead and get some rest," Kolorado replied. "I can't sleep anyhow."

I frowned hesitantly, and Kolorado scowled.

"You don't trust me?"

"It's not that," I said, and I explained about the campfire.

"You go on," Kolorado declared. "I'll keep an eye on things."

I frowned thoughtfully, and then I nodded.

"All right," I said. "I'll see you in the morning."

Kolorado nodded, and I walked towards the cabin.

Chapter forty-one

It was way past daylight when I finally woke up. I sat up abruptly, and I noticed that Cooper and Josie were just waking up too.

"It's late," Cooper said as he stretched.

"Too late," I frowned.

"Where's Kolorado?"

"He's supposed to be keeping watch," I replied.

We pulled our boots on and hurried outside, and Josie gasped in surprise.

Kolorado was stretched out on the ground beside the lean-to, and he was lying on his side.

We rushed over to him. Coop knelt down and rolled him over, and we heard a soft groan.

Kolorado had an arrow in his shoulder. It had gone all the way through, and the arrow was sticking out his back.

It was a bloody mess. Blood had run down his front and back, and his shirt was stained red.

Cooper shook Kolorado gently. He grunted and opened his eyes.

He looked startled. He tried to sit up, but Cooper stopped him.

"Take it easy," Cooper said. "It's us."

Kolorado stared up at Cooper with a confused look.

"What happened?" He asked, and his voice sounded hoarse.

"I was about to ask you that," I spoke up, and asked, "You don't remember?"

Kolorado blinked his eyes and thought for a moment.

"I was sitting by the lean-to, keeping watch, and then-," his voice trailed off.

"And then you fell asleep," I suggested.

Kolorado didn't reply. I sighed and looked at the corral, and I narrowed my eyes.

"We're missing two mules," I announced.

"The rifles," Cooper pointed. "They're gone!"

My face was emotionless as I looked at the lean-to. Just as Cooper had said, the crates were gone.

It was silent as we all thought about that.

"Don't say it," Kolorado finally said, and his voice sounded tired. "It's my fault."

"All right," I said. "I won't say it."

Cooper looked at me and frowned.

"It wouldn't have mattered if you were asleep or not," Cooper tried to be helpful. "You would have still been shot. What matters is that you're still alive."

"But I lost the trade goods," Kolorado muttered.

"You did," I agreed.

"How are we going to get the boy back now?"

"We'll find another way," I said.

Chapter forty-two

Josie took charge of the situation.

"Take him inside," she told us. "I fix."

Cooper looked at Josie and frowned hesitantly.

"How? The Indian way?"

"How else?" Josie grunted.

"I could pull the arrow out and stitch it up," Cooper suggested.

"My way is better," Josie replied stubbornly.

Cooper and Josie frowned at each other while I looked at Kolorado.

"It's your wound," I told him. "You decide."

"I'd rather have a woman fussing over me than you," Kolorado told Cooper.

Cooper nodded and shrugged.

"Fine by me," he said, and we picked him up and carried him inside.

Meanwhile, Josie walked out into the bushes, and she returned with two long, thin sticks.

"What are the sticks for?" Kolorado asked.

Josie didn't reply. Instead, she built the fire back up, and she whittled on the ends of the sticks. She finally seemed satisfied, and she stuck the whittled ends deep into the coals.

"This brings back too many painful memories," Cooper said, and he turned towards the door. "I'll be outside, looking for tracks."

"What's he mean about painful memories?" Kolorado asked after he was gone.

"I think you're about to find out," I replied.

Kolorado frowned while Josie peeled back his shirt and long johns. Then, she broke the arrow off, right behind the arrowhead. The movement hurt, and Kolorado grimaced in pain.

"This will hurt," Josie said, and she grabbed the arrow with both hands and yanked it out.

Kolorado screamed in pain. Josie's face was emotionless, but I couldn't help but grimace.

Blood flowed from both sides of the wound, but Josie didn't seem bothered. Instead, she broke the clean end of the arrow off, and she offered it to Kolorado.

"Bite down," she instructed. "It will help."

Kolorado was in great pain, but he managed to nod. Josie placed the end of the arrow in his mouth, and he clamped down.

Josie walked over to the fire and pulled out one of the sticks. The end was bright red and glowing. She blew softly on it, and it glowed even brighter.

"What are you going to do?" I asked as she walked over to Kolorado.

"I fix," she said, and she beckoned at me. "Hold him. Don't let him move."

I walked over and grabbed ahold. Josie nodded, and without warning she stuck the burning end into the wound.

It made a hissing sound as she forced it deep in the wound, and I could smell a burning smell. Kolorado screamed, and it was all I could do to hold him down. Then, he relaxed as he passed out.

It took a while for Josie to sear the front of the wound. Then, she grabbed the other stick while I rolled Kolorado over. He stirred momentarily, but then he passed out again and stayed unconscious until Josie had finished.

"I need mud from the creek," Josie told me. "It will help with the burning."

There was a bucket in the corner. I grabbed it, hurried down to the creek, and filled it with mud. I went back to the cabin, and Josie was smiling as she studied the wound.

"It doesn't bleed now," she said.

"That's wonderful," I said, and added, "I need some air. I'll be outside if you need anything."

123

Josie nodded, and I hurried out the door.

Chapter forty-three

I walked down to the lean-to and studied the horses, but my mind was on what Kolorado had just gone through.

I was still thinking about it when Cooper walked up. He glanced at me and noticed my disturbed look.

"How's Kolorado?"

"He's alive."

Cooper smiled and nodded.

"The worst of it is over now," he said.

"For Kolorado's sake, I sure hope so," I said.

"Now you know why I looked so peaked when you found me up here," Cooper said.

"I don't know what's worse. Searing the wound, or stitching it up."

"Be best not to get shot."

"Well, I learned one thing," I said.

"What's that?"

"Josie's a good woman," I declared.

"She sure is."

"And, you're lucky to have her."

"I am."

"Just don't ever make her mad again."

"I'll sure try not to," Cooper smiled.

"And I'll do the same," I said.

Cooper nodded. It was silent for a bit, and then Cooper changed the subject.

"I found the tracks, over there," he gestured to the west.

"How many?"

"Just one."

"That's all?"

"That's all," Cooper nodded, and added, "I think it was Rocca."

"But Kolorado was shot with an arrow," I pointed out.

"I didn't mention it before, but when you and Rocca were talking, I noticed that he had a bow and some arrows beside his bedroll."

"I didn't see that."

"You were busy."

"I was," I agreed, and I frowned as I thought on that.

"So, we can assume that Rocca stole our trade goods," Cooper surmised.

"I'd say so."

"And now, he's riding west towards the Apache camp."

"He also took Jug-head," I said.

"What?" Cooper looked startled.

I gestured at the corral.

"Jug-head is one of the mules that's missing."

"Poor 'ol Jug-head," Cooper smiled, and added, "It's a good thing we disabled those rifles when we did."

"Sure is."

"Course, Rocca doesn't know that we disabled them."

"No, he doesn't," I said thoughtfully.

"That could get him into trouble."

"It sure could," I agreed.

"I reckon we're going after him."

"My thoughts exactly," I said, and asked, "Do you think we can catch him before he reaches the Apache camp?"

Cooper thought for a moment.

"Not sure. Jug-head should help, but he has a big lead on us."

"Our only chance is if we leave Josie and Kolorado here," I said.

Cooper didn't like that, and he frowned thoughtfully.

"It's the only way," I said softly.

"I reckon it is," Cooper admitted. "But, I don't like it."

"You can stay," I offered. "I'll go after Rocca alone."

"No," Cooper shook his head. "I won't let you do that. Besides, I'm a better tracker."

I nodded, and it was silent for a bit.

"If we don't catch Rocca in time, No Worries might figure out that he's trading with damaged goods," Cooper said after a while.

"That would be a shame," I said.

We both smiled wolfishly at the thought, and we glanced at each other and noticed our wicked smiles.

"What's wrong with us?" Cooper wisecracked.

"Probably a lot more than we know," I replied.

Chapter forty-four

Cooper and I went back to the cabin. Kolorado was awake, and he was in an irritable mood.

"I see you're still alive," I said.

"It takes more than one arrow to bring this old buffalo down," Kolorado declared.

"How do you feel?"

"Like I've just been tortured," he scowled. "I didn't know a woman could be so rough."

Josie had just finished packing the wound with mud, and she paid no attention to him as she cleaned up things.

"You should see her when she's angry," I said.

Josie looked at me and frowned, and I smiled back. She tried to hold the frown, but then she broke and smiled back.

"It was Rocca who shot you," I told Kolorado. "Coop found his tracks, and he's headed for the Apache camp."

"What are you going to do?" Kolorado asked.

"Me and Coop are going after him," I declared, and Josie looked up sharply. "You and Josie will stay here."

"No. I go with you," Josie said.

"Josie, Kolorado can't stay here alone," Cooper spoke up. "He'll need your help."

Josie frowned, and it was silent for a long time.

"I'll stay," she finally said in a subdued voice.

"Our only chance is if we leave now," I spoke back up.

"I understand," Kolorado said, and added, "And don't worry about us. We'll be fine."

I nodded, and Cooper cleared his throat and looked at Josie.

"Soon as we leave, I want you to barricade this door," Cooper told her. "Don't open it for any reason, understand?"

Josie nodded, and Cooper gave her a hug and walked out the door. I started to follow him, but Josie reached out and stopped me.

"I am worried," she said.

"About what?"

"Cooper," she said. She hesitated and added, "And you."

"We'll be fine," I said reassuringly.

"He will not stop," she replied, "until the boy is safe."

"Neither will I," I declared.

"You are both very stubborn."

"Yes, ma'am."

"Do not let Cooper go to the Apache camp alone," she said. "They will kill him."

"If anybody could pull it off, it would be him," I replied. "He's got skills we ain't got."

"What skills?" Josie asked, confused.

"He's likeable," I explained.

Chapter forty-five

Josie followed me to the lean-to, and she stood there with a worried look while we saddled our horses.

A mule would slow us down, so we stuffed our saddlebags with all the canned goods that would fit, and then we climbed on our horses.

Cooper and Josie looked at each for a long time, and Cooper smiled gently.

"We'll be back," he said.

"You say that a lot."

"I know," he said, and he gestured at the cabin. "Remember what I told you."

Josie nodded, and she walked inside and shut the door. I looked at Cooper, and he nodded.

"Let's go," he said.

I nodded back, and we kicked up our horses and rode out.

Cooper found the tracks, and we fell into our routine. Cooper's eyes never left the ground, and mine never left the surrounding landscape.

By now it was late morning. The tracks were easy to follow, and we trotted briskly. We risked ambush, going that fast, but we had no choice.

The day passed quickly, and we rode until it got so dark that Cooper couldn't follow the tracks. There was a draw nearby, and we camped in the bottom.

We were now deep into Indian country, and it was too risky for a fire. We unsaddled and picketed our horses, and I pulled out some canned peaches and hardtack from my saddlebags. Cooper grabbed our canteens, and we sat on the ground and ate.

"Tracks getting any fresher?" I asked.

"Some," Cooper said, and added, "But not a lot."

"We aren't going to catch him," I said flatly.

"I'd say that's a good possibility," Cooper looked grim.

I nodded, and we frowned as we thought on that.

"Well, we'll come up with something," I said after a while.

"We always do," Cooper nodded.

"I can only imagine how terrified that boy is," I commented. "There's no telling what he's gone through these past few days."

"Josie would know," Cooper said. "If we get him back, she might be able to help him cope with things."

"Probably so."

Cooper nodded, and it was silent for a bit. As we sat there, I couldn't help but yearn for a hot cup of coffee.

"You want the first watch or the second?" Cooper broke the silence.

"Go ahead and get some sleep," I told him. "I'll keep watch for a while."

Cooper nodded and stood, and he walked over to his bedroll and rolled it out.

I frowned as I watched him uncoil his rope around his bed.

"Are you going to do that from here on out?" I asked with a frown.

"Any reason I shouldn't?"

"Sure. It makes you look foolish."

"I'd rather look foolish than be bit by a snake."

"But it doesn't make sense," I protested.

"Well, all I know is that I'm not the one who woke up with a rattler buzzing by my head."

I sighed and shook my head.

Chapter forty-six

We were up at daybreak. We chewed on some hardtack, and then we saddled our horses and rode out.

It was a muggy morning. And, even though it was cool, sweat streaked down our faces, and our shirts became damp.

"Sure is sticky this morning," I complained.

"Feels like it's going to rain, doesn't it?"

"It does," I admitted.

"Makes you wonder about those rain birds," Cooper said, and his eyes twinkled as he looked at me.

I scowled, and Cooper chuckled.

The morning passed smoothly. I kept a close eye out for Indians or an ambush, but I didn't see any sign of either.

The tracks started getting fresh around midday. However, we also knew that we were close to the Apache camp, so there was little hope in catching him now. And, even if we did catch him, we couldn't risk the sound of a shot.

There were trees all around us, and in front of us loomed a very steep ridge that went for miles. There was also a long ledge at the top.

"We might could spot the Apache camp from up there," Cooper pointed.

I thought on that and nodded.

"Be worth a look," I said.

It was too steep to ride, so we dismounted and tied our horses in amongst the trees. Cooper grabbed his spyglass, and we trudged to the top of the ledge.

It was a long, difficult climb, and we were out of breath when we reached the top. We were soaked with sweat, and flies buzzed around us. A few of them even flew up our noses, and we had to swat at them.

"These flies are driving me crazy," I said irritably.

"Means it's going to rain," Cooper said.

"Now *that* I've heard of," I said.

"It's getting dark in the west too," Cooper nodded at the sky.

I nodded, and then we looked below.

There was a valley in front of us, and the Apache camp was nestled beside a river that ran along the bottom. It was closer than we expected, and we squatted behind some brush.

"Well, there it is," Cooper said wryly.

"Sure is," I said, and it fell silent as we studied the layout.

The Indian camp was quite impressive. There were several hide-covered lodges pitched along the bank. Women, children, and dogs were all about, and there was plenty of laughter and chatter.

Their pony herd was on the other side of the river. They had a lot of horses, and we could see several Indian boys keeping watch.

There was a huge gathering of braves at a lodge on the outskirts of camp, and Cooper squinted through his eyeglass. A few seconds passed, and then he whistled.

"I see the boy," he said.

"Good," I said.

"Rocca's down there too," he continued. "No Worries is with him. Looks like he's trading the rifles."

"Is Wyatt all right?"

"I think so. He's sitting beside some other kids at the lodge on the outskirts of camp. I think that might be No Worries' lodge."

"Are his hands tied?"

"Not that I can see."

"They probably aren't too worried about him running off, this far from home," I figured.

"Probably so."

A rifle shot suddenly boomed out, and Cooper and I instinctively ducked.

"What was that?" I hissed.

"No Worries just fired one of the rifles," Cooper replied as he squinted through the eyeglass. "Probably making sure they work."

"I reckon he tried the right one," I replied, and added, "That about scared me to death."

Cooper smiled and nodded. He passed me the eyeglass, and I studied the camp for a long time.

"Interesting, No Worries' lodge being away from the others," I finally said.

"What's so interesting about that?"

"Do you reckon we could sneak up to the backside of that lodge at night?"

"No. It's too open down there. There's not any cover."

"Have any better ideas?"

Cooper thought for a moment.

"No."

There was a stirring below, and I looked through the spyglass again.

Rocca was mounted on his horse. He led Jug-head and the other mule, and they were packed down with pelts. He said something to No Worries, and then he kicked up his horse and rode out of camp.

We kept still and watched him. He rode to the top of the ledge about a half-mile from us, and he disappeared into the trees.

"Are we going after him?" Cooper asked.

"Catching him won't get Wyatt back."

"I reckon not."

"We'll wait and see what develops," I said.

Chapter forty-seven

We watched the camp for another hour. No Worries disappeared inside his lodge, but Wyatt never moved.

"The boy looks calm," I commented as I studied him through the eyeglass.

"I noticed that."

Suddenly, we heard a deep rumbling to the west. We glanced at each other and frowned.

"What was that?" Cooper asked.

"Mebbe it was a mile-or-more bird," I suggested.

We heard it again, and this time we could tell that it was thunder. We glanced up at the sky, and it was getting darker.

"It really is going to rain," Cooper said.

"Looks like it."

Another half hour passed, only this time we watched the sky more than we did the camp. Thunder kept rumbling in the west, and then it suddenly got very calm.

I looked down at the camp through the spyglass, and No Worries was outside, looking up at the sky. He said something to a squaw, and she gathered all the children, including Wyatt, and hurried them inside. Meanwhile, No Worries hustled around camp, and I could tell that he was talking to the other braves.

"They're getting ready for a storm down there," I commented.

"Yeah, and that storm is about to hit," Cooper said, and there was a worrisome sound to his voice.

The sky to the west had turned completely black. Lightning struck the ground, and the thunder was deafening. It started sprinkling, and the drops were big.

"We're about to get wet," Cooper said.

I nodded as I looked below.

All of the braves were running to their lodges, and I also noticed that there were no lookouts.

"Everybody's going inside," I pointed below.

"I'd go inside too if I had a place to go," Cooper said sourly.

"There's no lookouts," I said, and there was excitement in my voice.

Cooper looked at me and frowned.

"What are you thinking?"

"When the rain hits, I think we might could slip down there unnoticed, go into No Worries' lodge and whop him on the head, and grab Wyatt and make a run for it."

"What if it quits raining?"

"Then we'll die and take some Injuns with us."

Cooper scratched his jaw as he thought on that.

"Let's do it," he said.

I nodded, and we checked our weapons. There were still no lookouts below, so we started down.

We were about halfway down the ridge when the rain hit. It was the hardest rain I'd ever been in, and it felt like buckets of water being poured over us.

We were soaked within seconds. Just like that it was muddy and slick, and we had to be careful as we slogged along.

We were almost at the bottom when we heard a loud roar. We looked up, and water was pouring into the valley from the mountains.

"The valley's flooding!" Cooper yelled at me through the rain.

I nodded, and we trudged on.

We finally reached the bottom, and I was surprised at how deep the water was. Running water was up over our ankles, and the current was remarkably strong. It pulled at us, and it was hard to stand.

"I don't think we planned this out too well!" Cooper shouted.

"No," I shouted back. "We didn't!"

"Too late now!"

"Yes," I yelled. "It is!"

Chapter forty-eight

The rain was falling so hard that we could barely see as we made our way across the valley. However, that also meant that nobody could see us, so that was a good thing.

Our feet sunk in the mud with each step, and the strong current grabbed at us. But we managed to keep on our feet, and we finally reached the backside of No Worries' lodge.

The rain was still falling in sheets, and it was beating hard against the side of the lodge. I pulled out my knife, and I made a long cut in the tanned hide. The rain was so deafening that it didn't make a sound.

I looked at Cooper and nodded, and he nodded back. I took a big breath and stepped inside, and Cooper was behind me.

Water was running through the lodge, and we could hardly hear anything. It was very black inside, but the cut in the hide allowed a little light in.

I heard a surprised grunt, and No Worries appeared in front of me. He was startled, but he recovered quickly and grabbed for his knife.

With an easy movement, I palmed my Colt. I swung it hard, and I hit No Worries on the side of the head. He grunted, and I holstered my Colt as he fell.

He was out cold, and his face was in the water. I knelt beside him and lifted him up, and I leaned him against the side so he wouldn't drown.

The squaw and the children were huddled together in the corner. They seemed to be more terrified than hostile, but Cooper covered them with his rifle anyhow.

I spotted Wyatt. He looked scared, and he stared at us through wide eyes.

"Come here, Wyatt," I called out to him. "We're here to help."

The boy didn't move, and I frowned and looked at Cooper.

"Grab him!" I said.

Cooper walked over and picked him up. Wyatt started to fight back, but Cooper held on firmly.

"Stop it!" Cooper yelled. "We're here to help!"

Wyatt didn't say anything, but he stopped struggling as Cooper threw him on top of his shoulder.

"Let's go!" Cooper yelled at me.

I nodded. Cooper walked towards the cut in the hide, but I turned towards No Worries.

"What are you doing?" Cooper yelled at me.

I didn't reply as I knelt beside No Worries.

I grasped No Worries on the shoulder. I squeezed hard, and then I looked at the squaw, smiled, and followed Cooper outside.

It was still pouring rain, and by now the water was almost to our knees.

Suddenly, we heard some screams from camp. We looked, and a lodge was breaking up and was being swept away. Several Indians came outside and tried to help, but they were too busy to notice us.

I motioned at Cooper, and we trudged across the valley. The current was extremely strong, and we had to be careful with each step.

We finally reached the edge of the valley. We started climbing the ridge, and it was a relief to be heading to higher ground.

The rain finally started to lighten as we reached the top. I glanced below and noticed that several lodges had been swept away. The river beside the camp was roaring, and I could see some white rapids.

Cooper sat the boy down on the ground and looked him over.

"Are you all right?"

The boy just stared at him through wide eyes.

"Do you remember me, Wyatt? I'm Cooper. We met in Midway."

The boy nodded, but that was all.

"You're safe now, you understand?"

Again, the boy just nodded.

Cooper nodded back and looked at me.

"We'd best be going," Cooper said. "They'll be after us as soon as they find out what happened."

"I don't think so," I said, and I gestured below. "That river is still rising. I think they're cut off from their horses."

Cooper walked up beside me, and he nodded as he looked below.

"I think you're right."

"We'll be a long ways from here by the time that river goes down." I said.

"But they still might come after us on foot," Cooper warned.

"Let's be going then," I suggested.

Cooper nodded and picked up the boy, and we trudged back to where we had left the horses.

We were relieved to find them still there.

The horses were skittish, and we had trouble getting mounted. Cooper got on first, and I managed to get Wyatt up behind him. I climbed on my horse, and we took out.

We trotted briskly, and we put several miles between the Indian camp and us. Only then did we relax some.

"What'd you do back there?" Cooper asked me.

"No Worries counted coup against me once, so I returned the favor," I explained.

"Unless the squaw tells him, he won't even know it," Cooper objected.

"I'll know," I said.

Chapter forty-nine

Despite being soaked, we were in good moods as we rode along. We had Wyatt back, and that's all that mattered.

The ground was wet and slick, but we still managed a brisk trot. We made good time, and by dark we were roughly halfway back to the cabin.

We wanted to push on, but it was too muddy to ride in the dark. So, we holed up amongst some trees, and I pulled out some canned goods. Wyatt was hungry, and he tore into his food with a vengeance.

Afterwards, Cooper talked to him some, but he still wouldn't answer. However, he did nod his head every once in a while.

We sat there a while, and then Cooper and Wyatt turned in while I kept watch. Cooper relieved me around midnight, and come daylight we saddled up and pushed on.

The morning passed quickly. We were all a bit jumpy, but nothing happened.

It was late morning when we finally arrived at the cabin.

Cooper looked concerned as we rode up. I glanced at the corral, and I was relieved to see the horses and mules.

"Hello the cabin!" Cooper called out. "It's us!"

It was silent, and then the door opened. Josie stood in the doorway, and a huge grin crossed her face when she saw us.

"You are here!" She exclaimed.

"I told you we'd be back," Cooper smiled at her.

Josie spotted Wyatt, and she gasped in surprise. She rushed forward and helped Wyatt down, and she ignored Cooper as she led Wyatt inside.

Cooper frowned thoughtfully and looked at me.

"Now you know how I feel," I said.

Cooper snorted, and we dismounted and followed them inside.

Kolorado was lying on the ground in the corner. He tried not to show it, but I could tell that he was glad to see us.

"You got the boy back," he said.

"We did," I nodded.

"How did you manage to pull that off?"

"The rain helped."

"I told you it was going to rain," Kolorado looked proud.

"You were right," I said.

"We're still wet too," Cooper added, and he patted his damp shirt.

"How do you feel?" I asked Kolorado. "Are you queasy after losing all that blood?"

"Me? Queasy?" Kolorado scowled. "I've got the gut of a buzzard."

"You and your birds," I frowned, and added, "Well, if you can ride, I suggest we get going."

"Are they coming after us?" Kolorado asked.

"Probably not, but I see no reason to wait around and find out," I said.

"Me neither," Kolorado said, and he reached for my hand. "Help me up, and then we can go."

Cooper and I grabbed his hands and pulled him to his feet. He swayed a bit, but then he nodded.

"I'm fine," he said.

"We'll go saddle the horses," I said, and Cooper and I walked outside.

Cooper saddled Josie's horse, and I saddled Kolorado's. After that we packed the mules, and then we helped Kolorado get into the saddle. His face was pale, but he didn't say anything as we kicked up our horses and left out.

We could tell that Kolorado was in pain, so Cooper led out in a walk. Josie and Wyatt were next, followed by Kolorado and then me. Cooper led one of the mules, and I led the other one.

The nearest town was Landry, and the best way to go was to ride through Valverde's Pass. It was a steep descend, and Cooper followed an old trail.

The afternoon passed without incident. As it was getting dark, we reached the old trading post.

The trading post had once been a gathering spot for trappers to buy supplies, but that was before No Worries attacked and burned the place down. He destroyed everything, and all that was left were a few scattered burned logs.

The place had an eerie feel to it as we stopped and made camp.

We helped Kolorado over to a log and got him comfortable. Then, Cooper and Josie tended to the horses while I built a fire, put the coffee on, and started supper. Meanwhile, Wyatt sat beside Kolorado, and he watched us silently.

Once the chores were done, everyone gathered around the campfire.

I had gone two days without coffee, and my mouth salivated as we waited for the coffee to boil.

It was finally ready. I poured everyone a cup, and I cradled my cup and leaned back. I took a swig and sighed in contentment.

Supper was ready soon. We were hungry, and we tore into our meal with a vengeance. Afterwards, we drank some more coffee.

"Lotta memories here," I commented as we sat there.

"Yep," Cooper nodded. "This is where we killed the Oltman brothers."

"All except for Tom," I reminded. "I killed him in Midway during the range war."

"I remember that," Cooper nodded.

"This is also where you got shot in the hip the second time," I said.

"No, here it was the first time," Cooper corrected.

I thought for a moment and nodded.

"You're right," I said. "You've been shot so many times, it's getting hard to keep it straight."

Cooper frowned at me, and I smiled. Meanwhile, Kolorado grunted and shook his head.

"I declare. Every time we camp, you and Cooper start reminiscing on who was shot here, and who shot him," Kolorado said.

"I reckon we have," I admitted.

"Just how many men have you two killed?"

"A lot," I said.

***

We drank another pot of coffee, and then we turned in.

I had the first watch, and Cooper relieved me around midnight.

"Anything stirring out there?" Cooper asked as he walked up.

"Nope," I replied.

Cooper nodded, and I went over to my bedroll. I rolled it out, pulled my boots off, and crawled in. I was tired, and I was out soon as my head hit the ground.

Chapter fifty

A rifle shot woke me the next morning. I sat up abruptly, and my Colt was in my hand.

Everybody else was startled too, and I heard an alarmed cry from Josie.

Cooper was on his back, behind the log that he'd been sitting on. His face was pale, and I could see blood on his shoulder.

"Keep down!" I hissed at everyone, and I crawled over to him.

"Coop," I said tersely.

"I'm here," he said, and his voice sounded strained.

"Hit bad?"

"Not sure."

I peeled his shirt back while Josie crawled over.

"You're hit in the shoulder," I told him.

"I told you I always get shot up here," Cooper grimaced through clenched teeth.

I started to reply, but before I could someone yelled from below.

"Hello the camp!"

I looked over the log and spotted Rocca. He was leaning against a tree with his arms crossed.

"Morgan! Morgan Gant!" He yelled.

"Yes?" I shouted back.

"Come down, and I will let the others live!"

Kolorado and Josie looked at me with worried looks.

"What are you going to do, Yancy?" Kolorado asked in a hushed voice.

"I'm going to oblige him," I declared, and then I yelled below, "I'll be right down!"

I checked my Colt, and then I stood, walked over to my horse, and saddled him.

"Why don't you shoot him from here with your rifle?" Kolorado suggested. "He's close enough."

"That's not how I do things," I replied as I stepped into the saddle.

Kolorado didn't reply, and I looked at Josie.

"Take care of Cooper," I said.

"Be careful," Josie replied.

I nodded and kicked up my horse.

***

I rode down the hill, and I pulled up when I was about fifty feet away. I dismounted and tied my horse to a nearby bush.

Rocca walked forward a little, and he watched me with a scornful look.

The feeling came over me as I walked toward him. I could feel blood running through my veins, and my heart thumped steadily. I also felt a calmness and a readiness.

I stopped about twenty feet from him, and we faced up to each other. My gun hand hovered over my gun-handle, as did his.

"You shot my brother," I said.

A smirk crossed Rocca's face.

"I do not miss," he said.

"Neither do I," I said. It was silent, and I added, "Those rifles you traded; they were no good except for a few of them. They won't fire."

Rocca looked startled, and he narrowed his eyes.

"You lie."

"Tell you what. You ride back and see for yourself. No Worries would like that."

Rocca frowned as he thought on that.

Moving slowly with my left hand, I reached into my pocket, pulled out my Ranger's badge, pinned it on my vest, and gave it a little pat.

"My name is Yancy Landon," I said, and added, "I'm a Texas Ranger."

"No, you are Morgan Gant," Rocca said, but there was uncertainty in his voice.

"Sorry to disappoint you, but Morgan Gant is dead. So is Boyle."

"You lie."

"I killed him," I said. I let that sink in, and added, "The man who killed your father is dead."

Rocca was silent as he thought on that.

"You are Yancy Landon?" He finally said.

"I am."

"And you killed Gant."

"I did."

"I thank you for that."

"You're welcome," I said, and then I continued, "As a Texas Ranger, I'm arresting you for attempted murder and for trading rifles to the Injuns. Unbuckle your gun-belt."

Rocca looked amused.

"If I don't?"

"Then I'll shoot you."

"Nobody beats Rocca," he declared.

"I ain't nobody," I said.

"Maybe I kill you anyway," he said.

"You can try."

It was silent then, and we stared at each other. I stood still and waited for him to make the first move.

He chuckled softly, and then he grabbed for his Colt.

With an easy movement, I palmed my Colt.

Rocca had his Colt out too, but I fired as he brought it up. There was a loud thumping sound, and the bullet caught him in the belly. He staggered backwards but stayed on his feet as he tried to lift his Colt.

I fired again, and the bullet hit Rocca in his chest. He was flung backwards, and he hit the ground on his back. He kicked out a few times and made some gurgling sounds, and then he was still.

I watched him for a moment. Satisfied, I reloaded and holstered my Colt and walked back to my horse. I climbed into the saddle, looked at Rocca once more, and rode back up the hill.

Chapter fifty-one

I was relieved to see Cooper sitting up. He was leaning against a log, and he managed to smile as I rode in.

"I saw the whole thing," he said as I dismounted and walked over. "Rocca was good."

"He was."

"He almost beat you."

"But he didn't," I said, and asked, "You all right?"

"I got lucky. The bullet went all the way through. Near as Josie can tell, the bullet didn't hit anything important."

"That's good," I said, and then I glanced at his shoulder. It was bleeding, but not near as bad as Kolorado's wound had.

"A bullet makes a smaller hole than an arrow does," Kolorado spoke up.

"It does," I agreed, and I frowned as I looked around. "Where's Josie?"

"She's hunting for a stick," Cooper said, and he had a pained expression on his face.

I frowned thoughtfully.

"Well, good luck with that. I saw Rocca's mules down there, so I'm going to go get 'em, and while I'm down there I'll bury Rocca," I said.

"You ain't staying?" Cooper protested. "I might need some help. You know how Josie is."

"You'll be fine," I said, and Cooper scowled as I climbed back on my horse. "Will you be able to ride?" I asked.

"I can try."

I nodded.

"We'll leave as soon as Josie gets you patched up," I said.

Cooper nodded solemnly. I nodded back and kicked up my horse.

***

It took me an hour to get Rocca buried. After that, I picked up the mules and rode back up the hill.

Cooper was still leaning against the log. His shoulder was bandaged, and he looked like he was in pain.

"How'd it go?" I asked.

"How do you think?" Cooper scowled.

I smiled, and then I gestured at the mules.

"Look. You got Jug-head back."

"That's wonderful," Cooper said flatly.

"Both of these mules are also packed down with a lot of pelts," I added.

Cooper looked thoughtful as he studied the mules.

"Good looking pelts," he said.

"They are," I agreed.

"What are we going to do with them?"

I scratched my jaw.

"They should be worth a lot," I said.

"They sure should."

"If we sold them, we could use the money to help Wyatt," I suggested.

"Now that ain't a bad idea at all."

"It's settled then?"

Cooper nodded, and I glanced at Wyatt. He was watching us closely, but his face was emotionless.

"Well, are you ready to go?" I looked back at Cooper.

"Just get me on a horse," Cooper declared.

I smiled and nodded.

Chapter fifty-two

We limped into Landry three days later. It was slow going, and we were tired, dusty, and in need of a bath.

We received a few curious looks as we rode to the livery stable. It was late, and Kolorado's wife had already gone home.

I dismounted and helped Kolorado down while Josie helped Cooper. Next, I opened up the livery stable, and we unsaddled and fed our horses and mules.

"Can I go home now?" Kolorado asked when we were done.

I smiled.

"You can," I said, and I reached into my pocket, pulled out the pardon, and handed it to him. "I believe this is yours."

Kolorado nodded as he took it.

"The way it turned out, I really wasn't even needed," he grumbled.

"I reckon not," I said.

"To show there's no hard feelings, I'm going to let you three stay here tonight free of charge," Kolorado declared.

I glanced at Cooper and frowned thoughtfully.

"I appreciate the offer, but I think we'll get us a room at the hotel tonight," I said. "How does that sound, Coop?"

"A soft bed would be nice," Cooper said.

Kolorado grunted and shook his head. He muttered something as he limped towards the door, and I smiled as I watched him.

"Take care of yourself," I said.

"Sure. You do the same," Kolorado said, and then he walked out the door.

I looked at Cooper, and he smiled and shrugged.

"He ain't much for saying goodbye, is he?" Cooper said.

"No, he's not," I replied.

"Well, I don't know about you, but I could use a bath and a shave, and then I wouldn't mind eating some mystery stew over at the café," Cooper commented as we walked towards the door.

"And some coffee," I added.

"That too," Cooper said, and we headed towards the hotel.

***

An hour later, we sat around a table at the café. We had just finished supper, and we were drinking coffee. Wyatt liked coffee too, and he drank just as much as the rest of us.

"Well, it feels good to be alive," Cooper declared.

"Does," I agreed, and Josie and Wyatt nodded.

"There's one thing I don't understand," Cooper said.

"What's that?"

"Why did Rocca shoot me for?" Cooper complained. "I ain't the one who killed his father."

"I reckon he wanted to get our attention," I said.

"Couldn't he have just yelled or something?"

"It probably had something to do with his father," I explained.

"He wanted you to know what it felt like, to lose someone close," Cooper surmised.

"Something like that."

"So, this was all about revenge."

"I'd say so."

"And, it got him killed," Cooper declared.

"With a little help from me," I smiled.

Chapter fifty-three

We rested up for a day, and then we headed for Midway. Because of Cooper we had to ride slow, and it took us three days.

We caused quite a commotion as we rode into Midway. Folks crowded around us, and they all stared at the boy. There was some applause and even a few cheers. I looked around for Sheriff Wagons, but I didn't see him.

I didn't care much for all the attention, and Wyatt didn't like it either. He was scared, and he stuck by Josie's side. Several folks offered to take him, but we decided that he would stay with us.

The crowd finally broke up and left us alone. We tended to our horses, and then we went to the café and ate supper. After that, we went to our house. Josie fixed Wyatt a bed in the corner, and we turned in early.

***

It felt good to be in our own house, and we slept in a bit the next morning.

I made another pot of coffee after breakfast, and Cooper and I went out onto the front porch. I poured us both a cup, and we sat and watched the activity on the street. It was shady and cool and pleasant.

"I wonder where Sheriff Wagons is," Cooper said.

I took a swig of coffee.

"I'm sure he'll show up," I said.

"I haven't seen Judge Parker either."

"I heard last night that he's out of town on some business," I said.

Cooper nodded, and it was silent for a while. We drank some more coffee, and then I cleared my throat.

"How's Wyatt doing?" I asked.

"He still ain't talking much."

"That's probably why he's fitting in so well," I said wryly.

"He sure likes Josie," Cooper said as he ignored my comment. "They seem to have bonded."

"That's good."

"Josie understands what he's gone through. She wants to help."

"If anybody can, it'll be Josie," I said.

Cooper nodded and looked at me.

"Josie and I talked it over," he said. "She wants the two of us to finish raising him."

"You and me?"

"No, me and Josie," Cooper frowned at me. "Course, you're part of the family too. You'll be Uncle Yancy."

"Are you sure about this?"

"It's what Josie wants, and I want what she wants."

"Shouldn't we try to find out if he has any family first?"

"Josie asked, and he said he doesn't."

"Wyatt actually talked?"

"He'll talk to Josie when nobody else is around," Cooper explained.

I nodded thoughtfully but didn't say anything.

"This will be good for Josie," Cooper continued. "It'll make her feel like she's doing something worthwhile."

"I reckon it's settled then," I said. It was silent, and I added, "I'll help any way I can."

Cooper nodded, and we drank some more coffee.

It was real peaceful, sitting there, and we were in no hurry. Another hour passed, and we spotted some movement down the street.

I squinted against the sun, and I frowned when I recognized Jessica. She had spotted us, and she was walking towards us.

Cooper saw her too, and he looked at me and smiled.

"Looks like Jessica is back from Empty-lake," he said.

"I see that."

"She's coming this way too."

"She is," I said, and already I could feel a nervous feeling building up inside me.

"This should be interesting," Cooper said.

I scowled, but Jessica arrived before I could say anything.

It was silent while we looked at each other. Jessica looked nervous too, and she tried to smile.

"Hello, Yancy," she said.

"Jessica."

"I just heard what you and Cooper went through. That was very courageous, getting that boy back."

"Just doing our job."

"I also heard that you killed a lot of men."

"I only killed some of them," I corrected. "Cooper here killed a couple."

"How did that feel, killing all those men?" Jessica looked at me through wide eyes.

"Necessary," I said.

Jessica frowned, and it was silent while we searched for words.

"How was your trip?" I changed the subject.

"It was unpleasant. I'm glad to be back," Jessica said.

"And how is Lee?" I couldn't help but ask.

"I don't know, and I don't care how Lee is," Jessica declared, and her eyes flashed angrily.

I was startled. I glanced at Cooper and looked back at Jessica.

"I'm sorry to hear that."

"I'm not," Jessica declared.

I frowned as I thought on that, and then Jessica changed the subject.

"Tomorrow's Sunday," she said.

"Yes, ma'am."

"Would you like to ride out and have supper with us tomorrow evening?"

I was startled again, but I recovered quickly.

"I sure would," I said.

"It's settled then," Jessica said, and she looked at Cooper. "You and Josie and Wyatt are invited too."

"I'll talk with Josie," Cooper said.

Jessica nodded and looked back at me.

"I'll see you tomorrow evening then."

"Yes," I said. "You will."

Jessica smiled, and she turned and walked down the street.

Soon as she was gone, I looked at Cooper.

"Well!" I exclaimed.

"That's a deep subject for such a shallow mind," Cooper smiled.

"It sounds like Jessica doesn't care for Lee's company anymore," I said as I ignored Cooper's comment.

"But she obviously cares for yours," Cooper said.

"I wonder what Lee did?"

"I wouldn't worry about that," Cooper replied.

"Why not?"

"You're having supper with Jessica," Cooper reminded. "That means you're going to have a long, drawn out conversation."

I frowned as I thought on that.

"This could be difficult," I said.

"I know," Cooper replied.

Epilogue

Cooper and I ran out of coffee, so I went inside and made another pot. Soon as it was ready, I went back outside and refilled our cups.

As I sat back down, I spotted Sheriff Wagons walking up the street. Cooper saw him too, and he glanced at me and smiled.

We were silent as Wagons walked up and stopped in front of us. He puffed his chest out and tried to look important.

"You're back," Wagons said.

"We are," I agreed.

"I wasn't here yesterday. I was gone on sheriff's business."

Cooper and I nodded and smiled.

"After you left, I went out and brought the Walden's wagon in," Wagons said.

"That's good," I replied.

"It was the right thing to do."

"Being right is never wrong," I said.

Wagons liked that. I knew by his expression that he was trying to remember my saying, probably so he could use it for his own.

"I heard you got shot again," Wagons looked at Cooper.

"I did," Cooper nodded.

"Well, I'm glad you're all right."

"So am I," Cooper said.

Wagons nodded and looked at me.

"You were once the law in this town," he declared.

"I was."

"But, you're not anymore," Wagons pointed out.

"I'm not," I agreed.

"I'm the law now," Wagons declared.

"You are," I nodded.

"This is my town now, and I don't want any trouble."

"Wagons," I said flatly.

"Yes, Yancy?"

"You can leave us now."

Wagons blinked in surprise. He opened his mouth, but couldn't think of anything to say. He stood there a moment, and then he turned and walked down the street. His movements were abrupt and jerky.

"How did he ever manage to kill Stew Baine?" I asked softly as we watched him.

Cooper didn't reply. Instead, he just chuckled.

***

Soon as Wagons left, Cooper pulled out his tobacco pouch while I poured myself another cup of coffee.

Cooper packed his pipe and lit it while I poured three spoonfuls of sugar in my coffee. I stirred and took a swig while Cooper took a deep puff.

"So, what happens next?" Cooper asked.

"I'm going to have supper with Jessica," I said.

Cooper looked at me and frowned.

"I meant with Ike."

"Oh," I said. "Well, there's not much we can do for a while."

"I reckon we accomplished what we set out to do," Cooper figured.

"That is correct," I agreed. "Ike doesn't know it, but he's no longer trading rifles with the Injuns."

"Instead, he's trading with us," Cooper said.

"Yep," I nodded, and continued, "I plan to sit here on this porch and drink coffee for a few weeks, and then we'll go meet Brock."

"I didn't like Brock. He was too cocky."

"You can tell him that, if'n you want," I offered.

"I think I will."

I smiled and asked, "Will Josie and Wyatt be coming with us?"

"They're not staying here. Josie doesn't like being in town."

"Living out in the open seems to fit her better," I said.

"Fits me better too."

"Are you sure you want to bring Wyatt along? Things are bound to get dangerous."

"Wyatt will be fine," Cooper declared. "He's tough."

"Well, I ain't got any objections," I said. I smiled, and added, "That is, long as Josie doesn't get the notion to cook for us again."

Cooper scowled at me, and then we both chuckled.

To be continued...

About the Author

Born in West Texas, Tell Cotten is a seventh generation Texan. He comes from a family with a ranching heritage and is a member of the Sons of the Republic of Texas. Besides writing, he is also in the cattle business, and he resides in West Texas with his wife, Andi, and their two children.

Tell has enjoyed writing from an early age, and he also has a great love of the history of the west. YANCY is his fifth novel in The Landon Saga series.

You can contact Tell at his website; http://tellcotten.wordpress.com/ and you can follow him on twitter at @TellCotten or on Facebook.

Acknowledgements
I would like to thank my wife and family for all their help and support. Without them this wouldn't be possible.

I'd also like to thank Bill for the fantastic drawing, and thanks to Mike for putting the cover together.

And lastly, I'd like to thank Melissa for all her advice, help, and hard work.

Enjoy this excerpt from Tell Cotten's upcoming novel:

Lee
Book six in The Landon Saga series

"Lee Mattingly," a cold, stern voice said.

The voice came from behind, so I stopped in the street. I turned around slowly, and my gun-hand hovered naturally over my gun handle.

Yancy Landon stood in front of me. His face was emotionless, and he looked ready to draw. I also noticed a Texas Ranger badge pinned on his vest.

The wind was blowing some, and dust swirled around us.

"Hello, Yancy," I smiled.

"Lee."

"You're a Texas Ranger now?"

"I am."

"How did that happen?"

"It happened," Yancy said, and declared, "You're under arrest."

"Don't think I want to be arrested today," I replied.

"I don't care what you want."

"Where's Cooper?" I asked.

"He's around."

I nodded. With my left hand I reached up and scratched my jaw, and I smiled at Yancy.

"What are you doing here, Yancy?"

"I could ask you the same thing."

I nodded and smiled sadly.

"I messed things up."

"I can see that."

"Have you seen Jessica?" I asked.

"Yes."

"How is she?"

"Fine."

I smiled and chuckled.

"You've never been one to talk much," I said.

Yancy ignored my remark.

"I'm taking you in, Lee."

"No," I shook my head. "You're not."

"I don't want to kill you."

"I know," I said softly, and added, "I think we've both known that someday, it would come to this."

"Unbuckle your gun belt," Yancy tried again.

"Can't."

"Why not?" Yancy looked at me hard.

"There's always been an unanswered question between us," I explained.

"What's that?"

"Who's best."

"That's a bunch of foolishness," Yancy retorted.

"It ain't for me."

Yancy glared at me, and I smiled back. Yancy studied me a moment more, and he narrowed his eyes.

"You do what you think best then," Yancy said.

I nodded.

"If you live, tell Jessica I'm sorry," I said.

"Sorry for what?"

"She'll understand."

Yancy nodded, and it fell silent.

My heart thumped as we stared at each other. Several seconds passed, and then we grabbed for our Colts.

Coming soon from Solstice Publishing

For an announcement of the release, you can follow Tell Cotten's website: http://tellcotten.wordpress.com/. You can also follow him on twitter at @TellCotten, or on Facebook.